THE SLUM REAPER

Esther & Jack Enright Mystery
Book Four

David Field

SAPERE
BOOKS

THE SLUM
REAPER

Published by Sapere Books.

11 Bank Chambers, Hornsey, London, N8 7NN,
United Kingdom

saperebooks.com

ISBN: 978-1-912546-77-0

Chapter One

Esther Enright leapt from the platform of the horse bus before it had even come to a halt at the stop outside the London Hospital in Whitechapel Road. If she even realised that she was back in her old haunts, she had more urgent matters on her mind as she ran as fast as her long skirts and heavy outdoor boots would allow, across the cobbled forecourt, through the imposing glass double doors and up to the reception desk. A serious-looking middle-aged nurse lowered her spectacles to regard her with disapproval as Esther stood before the desk, panting heavily and with sweat rolling down from the brim of her bonnet; it was a hot afternoon in early May, 1894, and Esther, although fit, was no athlete.

'I'm Mrs Enright and I believe that my husband was admitted late this morning? Police Constable Jackson Enright?'

The receptionist looked down at her notes, adjusting her spectacles several times as she traced her finger down the numerous entries in her own deplorable handwriting. As she waited in mounting fear and frustration, Esther looked at the depressing sights all around her — people with various parts of their anatomies heavily bandaged and a woman being assisted towards the exit as she leaned heavily on a walking stick. Someone covered in blood was being carried in on some sort of stretcher and nurses in starched uniforms were running towards it in order to render what initial assistance they could. Esther shuddered and wondered if Jack had entered the hospital this way.

'He's probably in the operating room by now,' the receptionist advised her, breaking into her thoughts. 'It's on the first floor, up those stairs ahead of you.'

Esther thanked her hastily as she took off, holding her skirts above her knees with one hand as she took the stairs two at a time. On the first landing a sign directed her to the left and she raced down the hallway, past nurses pushing stretchers on wheels or carrying rolls of bandages and suspicious looking pots covered over with cloths. Almost at the end of the hall was a large sign suspended from the ceiling with an arrow indicating that behind the double heavy-rubber doors to the right was the 'Operating Room'.

Esther was querying in her own mind whether she was allowed beyond those doors when a dark haired young man with a fashionable drooping moustache came out dressed in white overalls with something draped around his neck that looked like a set of horse brasses. He looked into her face and smiled.

'You look a little lost, Miss.'

'Mrs,' Esther insisted. 'Mrs Enright. You have my husband Jackson in there, I'm told. Is he going to be alright?'

'That depends upon whether or not he was thinking of dancing a jig in the immediate future,' the man replied, smiling reassuringly. 'I'm Dr Melton and I just fixed your husband's broken leg.'

'Is that all?' Esther asked as the relief flooded over her.

'Isn't that enough? I'm advised that Mr Enright is a serving police officer, but he won't even be fit for points duty for the next few months. He'll need to walk with the aid of a stick even when the fracture has fully healed and in cold weather it will ache for the rest of his life. But yes, could have been worse I suppose.'

'Can I go in and see him?'

'Not through there you can't, unless you want a very sudden and shocking introduction to surgical operations. He'll be one floor up in "Male Surgical" by now, I imagine, but he'll probably still be coming out from under the influence of the chloroform and may well be talking gibberish.'

'At least that'll prove that he's back to normal,' Esther chirped as she headed for the stairs at the end of the hallway. A few seconds later she remembered her manners and turned with the intention of thanking the doctor, but he had disappeared.

Two minutes after that she'd persuaded the sister on duty at the desk in the centre of the ward that police officers injured in the course of duty were entitled to special visiting times and was in the process of carrying a chair to the side of Jack's bed halfway down the ward when he opened his eyes and smiled groggily.

'I'm afraid my suit trousers have probably had it.'

'What happened?' Esther asked as she kissed him gently on the forehead and sat down, taking his free hand in hers.

'I fell under a horse,' he advised her, then closed his eyes and passed out cold. Esther remained where she was, reassuring herself that she could still see the bedclothes moving up and down in a gentle motion, until she heard a familiar voice arguing with the sister at the ward desk.

'Not only am I his senior officer, I'm also his uncle. Unless you want to be arrested for not being in possession of a heart, I insist on seeing him.'

'Over here, Uncle Percy!' Esther called across to him and the thin-faced older man gave her a wave of recognition and walked over, armed with a chair that he purloined from alongside an adjoining empty bed.

'He woke up just a moment ago,' Esther told him with a relieved smile, 'and he muttered some nonsense about a horse, then passed out again. I think he's alright, though.'

'It wasn't nonsense,' Percy assured her, 'and your husband's a hero.'

'What do you mean?'

'He was down in Limehouse apparently, waiting by a paddy wagon while some chinamen were being loaded in after they'd been arrested for running a pipe house. One of their supporters threw a firecracker in an effort to divert attention and the horse pulling the wagon took fright and bolted. There were some children further down the street, playing hopscotch and they were right in the path of the horse, so Jack made a grab for its reins and hung on. The horse pulled up and Jack fell under its hooves, where he came off second best. That's what they're saying around the Yard, anyway.'

'The bobby who came to our door to tell me Jack was in here said something about a riot,' Esther said, 'and I naturally assumed that he was badly injured. Turns out he's only broken a leg.'

'The riot came after two of the men were thrown out of the paddy wagon and made a run for it, assisted by many sympathisers. Order was fully restored with the aid of billy-clubs, or so I hear.'

'Will Jack suffer any loss of pay while he's recovering?' Esther asked nervously. 'Only now that we have two more to feed...'

Percy shook his head reassuringly.

'No, but once he's able to walk again he'll be put on light duties, so there'll be no more overtime opportunities for a while. The Met looks after its injured men, particularly its heroes.'

'Will they pay for a new suit?' came a weak voice from the bed.

Percy grinned down at him.

'Nothing wrong with you, obviously. Inspector Pennington sends his best wishes, by the way.'

'Nice of him, in the circumstances,' Jack conceded sarcastically, 'but at least I've seen the last of drug dens for a while. It's been almost three years and I was hoping to ... oh damn!'

'Jack!' Esther protested, as she looked round for the source of his outburst. As she followed Jack's horror-stricken gaze she saw a group of three men smiling and nodding in their direction, while the ward sister who'd been so frosty in her manner towards Esther was now doing all but curtsey.

Percy stood up sharply and edged as far away from Jack's bed as he could, whispering 'The bloody Commissioner!' as the three men approached it.

'The bloody Commissioner indeed,' the man in the centre confirmed as he leaned down towards Jack. 'We've never met,' he said, smiling, 'but I'm Colonel Bradford, and these two gentlemen are senior administrators of the hospital. I'm here, first of all, to ensure that you're getting the best available treatment, secondly to assure you that you'll be transferred to light duties — probably in Records somewhere — and finally, but most importantly, to advise you that I'm considering recommending you for a medal from the Queen, or perhaps the Home Secretary.'

'I'll definitely be needing that new suit,' Jack said, grinning up at Esther.

'Is this delightful lady your wife?' the Commissioner enquired.

Jack nodded. 'Her name's Esther.'

The Commissioner smiled. 'I'm sure that Mrs Enright can speak for herself, Constable. So, tell me, madam, how does it feel to be married to a real life hero?'

'I'm just glad he wasn't more badly injured,' Esther replied. 'We have two children, you see.'

'Yes, I quite understand,' the Commissioner assured her. 'Have no fear that your brave husband will suffer any loss in income. In fact, he may well qualify for a special injuries bonus. How long have you been with the Met, Constable?'

'Coming up to eight years in all, sir, the past six with the Yard.'

'And no promotion since you joined?'

'No, sir, but I'm still only twenty-six.'

'You may be aware that one of my policies has been to reward loyal service and promote men while they're still active enough to be of value. I see no reason why we can't consider elevating you to Sergeant.'

'Thank you, sir!' Jack spluttered, while to one side Percy grinned approvingly.

Ten minutes later, after obtaining all the detail he could from Jack regarding the accident that had hospitalised him, the Commissioner took his leave and it fell silent for a moment around Jack's bed.

'When do you think they'll let you out?' Percy asked. 'We'll need to get your mother to organise a celebration party.'

'A pity I had to do battle with a horse to get promoted,' Jack muttered.

'We'll need to sort you out with a new suit. I think I'd like to see you in dark brown this time.'

'Like the mess he's always getting himself into,' Percy chuckled, then straightened his face when he caught the look on Esther's.

Chapter Two

Alice Bridges was waiting with an anxious face as Esther opened the front door and gave her a reassuring smile.

'Jack's fine — just a broken leg, but I might need you to help out more regularly while I visit him in hospital. There's no way of knowing when he'll be let out and even then he'll be hobbling around on a walking stick, but at least he'll be home to look after the children while I do the shopping. Thank you *so* much for stepping into the breach today — I don't know what I'd have done without you.'

'Think nothing of it, dear,' Alice assured her with a warm smile. 'I'm only one floor up whenever I'm needed and I love children, as you know. Lily's such a sweet child and Bertie's a real treat to play with now that he's starting to talk. So, any time — you only have to ask. In fact, when Jack's home I need to ask his advice about another young person. One who's not so fortunate to have two remaining parents.'

'Put the pan on for some tea while I go and reassure the children that Mummy's still around and then you can tell me all about it,' Esther offered. 'There are some ginger biscuits left in the tin, I think — unless Jack ate them all while I wasn't looking.'

She poked her head round the door to the children's bedroom, where three-year-old Lily sat, organising a tea party for her dolls, while Bertie looked up with his entrancing smile that was an heirloom from his father and verbally acknowledged the entrance of 'Momma'.

'I hope you were good for Auntie Alice?' Esther demanded and they both beamed up at her. 'You two carry on being good for a little while longer, then it's fish for dinner.'

Bertie responded with 'fidge' without breaking the smile.

Back in the kitchen Esther helped herself to a ginger biscuit and sat down at the table before adding milk to the tea that Alice had taken the liberty of pouring her.

'So, what did you want Jack's advice on?' she asked.

Alice's face fell. 'It's probably nothing, dear, but I'm very worried about my niece Emily, my late sister's daughter. She works as a governess in this big old house in Hampstead and she and I used to exchange letters regularly. She's got no other family left, you see. My sister died only late last year and shortly after that her father was — well, not to put too fine a point on it, he was murdered. So, she had to go out into the world on her own and since she'd had a half decent education in one of those new Board Schools, she was able to get this governess's position to the family of a very successful solicitor and his wife. She seemed reasonably content there, to judge by her letters and what she used to tell me when we met up for little picnics by the lake on the local heath. She missed her old boyfriend, I know and she'd get a little teary whenever we talked about him, but that's no good reason why she should take herself off like that.'

'Like what?' Esther asked as she bit into another ginger biscuit, then closed the tin when Alice indicated with a shake of the head that she didn't want one.

'Well, like I said, we'd exchange letters every week, regular as clockwork. When I hadn't received one for a couple of weeks I just put it down to her being laid up with the 'flu or something, but when it reached three weeks I went up in person to the house she worked at. They all knew me, of course, from when

I used to call in and collect Emily for our little picnics on her days off, but this time when I appeared at the front door there was no answer, although I think I saw one the lace curtains moving at the front windows. Anyway, I went around to the scullery door at the back and spoke with the cook, who told me that Emily had taken off with her latest boyfriend and that if she dared to show her face at the house again she'd find she'd been sacked. Then the cook closed the door in my face.'

Esther reached out a reassuring hand towards Alice, whose own hand had begun to tremble slightly.

'I wouldn't worry, Alice, honestly. How old's your niece?'

'She turned twenty-three only a few weeks ago. March, it was. We went walking around the ponds as usual, then I took her for tea at that lovely cafe on the main road.'

'You know what young women are like these days. *Very* independently minded. In fact, it's only a few years since I was her age and I was obliged to earn my own living. I was also an orphan like her and when Jack came into my life I just clung to the hope that somehow we'd always be together. Now look at us — married for four years and with two children. You may have to resign yourself to the fact that she's expecting a child of her own by this boyfriend she's run off with and is probably too ashamed and embarrassed to contact you. But at least, if that's the case, she'll be safe and well.'

Alice looked doubtful. 'I don't know if that'll be the case, dear, but thank you for trying to lift my spirits. I know Emily, you see, and she's not the sort to fall for a man's charms that easily and be coaxed into running away.'

'But you said she'd had to leave a boyfriend behind from her old life?'

'Yes, a boy called Tommy, who lived back in Shoreditch and grew up in the next street from Emily and her parents. A fine strong boy who works as a roof tiler — at least he used to — and the two of them had known each other all their lives.'

'So, do you want Jack to have your niece listed as a missing person? I believe that the Met do that sort of work, or he may be able to recommend one of those private enquiry agents.'

'Do you think he'll agree to help?'

'We can only ask him, can't we? But once he gets home, I imagine that he'll have to rest for a while before he's allowed to go back to work.'

Two weeks later, Jack limped like a toy soldier up two flights of stairs, then stopped for breath and a few quiet curses while Esther used her key to unlock the front door. Alice smiled, welcomed him home, assured them that Lily and Bertie had been the epitome of good behaviour and took herself back upstairs to her rooms on the top floor. Jack knelt down gingerly on the hall carpet in order to receive the full force of Lily's charge towards him with a joyful shout of 'Daddy' and a flying embrace that nearly knocked him backwards. Then it was into the children's bedroom, where Bertie had once again escaped from his playpen and was making a determined bid for freedom on tottering legs towards the bedroom door.

'He's learned to walk all too quickly,' Esther complained.

'At least *he* can use both legs,' Jack complained grumpily as he lurched towards the kitchen with the aid of the strange device with which he'd been issued on his discharge from the hospital — a padded armrest with a leg that went all the way down to the floor. He was under strict instructions to return it to the London Hospital as soon as he could walk with only the aid of the walking stick to which he hoped to be able to convert with the minimum of delay. He dreaded going back to duty at the Yard looking like the well-described Long John

Silver. If he hobbled back to work in his current condition he could expect enquiries regarding the health of his missing parrot.

Esther laid out the tea things and announced proudly that there was some of Jack's favourite iced bun to go with it.

'Food fit for a hero?' Jack quipped with his old grin.

'For how long do you intend to play that particular card?' Esther reached up to the cupboard for the cake. 'I promised Alice that you'd do something for her.'

'What's the matter? Has she been caught running a bawdy house upstairs?'

'It's a bit more serious than that, I'm afraid.' Esther cut the cake and began to pour the tea as she passed on Alice's worries regarding her niece, Emily.

Jack frowned. 'We don't run a lost dog service at the Yard. If the girl's run off with her boyfriend, there's nothing we can do, given that she's over the legal age for that sort of thing. And if we do find her and try and persuade her to at least contact Alice, we may be accused of interfering in something that's none of our business. The Commissioner would not be amused, particularly if she complained to the newspapers, and then you could wave goodbye to my promotion. I can try and check that she's not dead, but beyond that there's precious little I can do, particularly if I'm stuck behind a desk.'

'What about Uncle Percy?'

'Forget it. He's up to his armpits in a whole string of murders in Bethnal Green. But that reminds me — he was planning on paying us a visit as soon as I was discharged from hospital. It seems that Mother's made him personally responsible for ensuring that I make a quick and full recovery.'

'Has she now?' Esther mused thoughtfully. 'That gives me an idea.'

'You're not normally so enthusiastic in your welcomes,' Percy observed as Esther sliced the roast lamb and ensured that he got four thick slices.

'No wonder,' Esther retorted, 'since you have this terrible habit of getting Jack involved in your cases at considerable risk to himself. And you've been known to drag me in as well from time to time. Though Jack can hardly involve me in his latest investigation, since it's all to do with a missing governess in Hampstead.'

'I haven't said I'll take the matter on yet,' Jack attempted to protest, before the look in Esther's eyes suggested that silence might be the best policy on his part.

'Hampstead?' Percy queried. 'That's "S" Division and almost off the Met's map.'

'That's the woman's last known address,' Esther told him. 'She's Alice Bridges' niece — you know, Alice upstairs, who helps mind the children?'

'I can well imagine why you'd want to keep in her good books,' Percy agreed, 'but are you back at work already?' he asked Jack with a look of concern.

'Yes, he is,' Esther intervened before Jack could say otherwise. 'Not officially, of course — he's doing this as a private job for our very obliging upstairs neighbour.'

'The Yard doesn't do "private jobs",' Percy replied. 'And Jack's supposed to be resting until he can make a complete recovery and return to his *official* duties.'

'This won't wait, I'm afraid,' Esther replied determinedly. 'Alice is beside herself with worry and can't get any satisfactory answers from the people her niece used to work for.'

Percy looked deeply concerned. 'Jack, you must understand that I can't let you do this. Your mother will have my guts if I let you tramp the outer northern suburbs on one leg. God alone knows how long it would set back your recovery and I'm supposed to be looking after your welfare.'

'This matter's too urgent,' Esther insisted, 'and Jack's promised Alice.'

'If it's that important,' Percy suggested, 'why don't I do it? My current investigations in Bethnal Green have hit so many brick walls that I'm beginning to suspect the local force of deliberate obstruction. I could probably spend an afternoon or so enquiring about this young woman you mention, and then Jack can stay home and rest. What do you say, Jack?'

'If you insist,' Jack replied weakly, intrigued by the way that events were turning out, 'but you'll need more details from Alice.'

'I thought you'd already got those?' Percy said suspiciously.

'Early days,' Jack explained. 'I'd only agreed in principle. Shall we invite Mrs Bridges down to give us more information?'

An hour or so later, Alice Bridges made her farewells, tearfully thanking Percy for undertaking to make enquiries concerning her missing niece. Percy also made his excuses and left, and as Jack closed the front door behind him he smiled and kissed Esther on the nose.

'You should be in the Detective Branch, you scheming hussy, you! Now, since the children appear to be asleep, let's test the limitations of my broken leg, shall we?'

Chapter Three

The following afternoon, cursing his over-eager nephew and his persuasive wife, Percy realised that he had probably been the victim of a confidence trick. But as a childless man himself, if you discounted the years he'd spent bringing up his dead brother's son, Jack, Percy had a soft spot for young people and he knew how Alice must be worrying about her missing niece. Even in leafy suburbs like Hampstead, horrible things could happen to young ladies who lacked street experience.

Number twenty-seven Heath Street certainly looked like the sort of establishment where one could remain ignorant of life in the real world that Percy had been policing for over thirty years. Four stories high, in the sort of dressed stone that had been very popular when Percy's own father had been trotting through the Essex countryside in his buggy, dispensing medicine and health advice to the wealthy, the place probably had four main bedrooms of its own, in addition to a clutter of 'servants' rooms' on its uppermost floor. There was a detached building off to the left and the sweeping semi-circular drive up which he was crunching confirmed the suspicion that whoever owned it probably employed his own coachman. The whole place reeked of upper-middle-class privilege, and although Percy was not given to those new 'progressive' political policies that the newspapers devoted so much space to, he couldn't help contrasting what lay in front of his eyes with the stews with their stinking back courts, their vermin ridden single rooms housing families of eight and their sullen resentful occupants that constituted his normal places of constabulary enquiry.

He pulled the bell rod that hung from the front door and somewhere inside it sounded as if the faithful were being summoned to Sunday prayer. When nothing happened the first time, he tried again and turned slightly to his left to monitor the lace curtain on the bay window. When it twitched slightly to betray the presence of a heavy breather on the other side, he extracted the wallet containing his police badge and placed it firmly against the glass with a weak, resigned smile. The sound of heavy door bolts being withdrawn heralded the opening of the door and there stood a 'tweenie' in her black dress with matching starched white apron and cap. Whoever occupied this mansion clearly preferred to employ a 'between maid' rather than a butler to deal with unwelcome police officers.

'Detective Sergeant Enright, Scotland Yard,' he announced, his badge held high in the air. 'I'd like to speak to your employer, if I may.'

'The Master's out fer the day, but the Mistress is in the drawing room,' the girl informed him as she stepped backwards in a non-verbal invitation to enter. He did so, making a big display of wiping his feet on the inside doormat before following meekly into the room on the left of the hall, from which his arrival had been surveilled. A tall, elegantly-dressed lady rose from her chair by the window, put down her book and asked his business as she looked him up and down in the manner of one inspecting a school child. She was, Percy surmised, in her mid to late thirties and time had been good to her. Or at least, someone had, since she had lost neither her youthful beauty nor her slender figure.

'I've been asked to enquire into the current whereabouts of a Miss Emily Broome, who I believe was, until recently at least, employed by you as a governess.'

'And what makes you think she is no longer employed by us?' the woman replied in a voice that was pure Mayfair.

'You *are* Mrs Mallory, I assume?'

She nodded gracefully as if accepting a bouquet from a loyal admirer.

'Millicent Mallory, that's correct. My husband Spencer is attending to his London practice at this hour, but I believe that I may speak for him when I express our disappointment at the circumstances in which Emily came to leave our service. That will be all thank you, Jane,' she advised the maid, who bowed slightly and oozed backwards out of their presence.

'Why were you disappointed, might I ask?' Percy enquired, since it seemed to be expected of him.

'Do you have children, Inspector?'

'Sergeant. And no, I don't.'

'Well, we have two, and to lose a governess with no prior notice is the height of inconvenience, apart from being ethically inexcusable. She was here the evening before and gone the following morning. No note, nothing — although she did at least have the decency to leave her room tidy.'

'When was this, exactly?'

'Sometime in the first week of April. It's now almost June and we haven't yet found a suitable replacement. It's really becoming intolerable.'

'Do you happen to know of any particular reason for her unannounced departure?' Percy asked.

'None whatsoever that warrants any sensible consideration. She was generously remunerated, she had her own room, she was very good with the children and so far as I was led to believe, she got on tolerably well with the other staff.'

'I heard a suggestion that she may have taken off with a young man.'

'You've presumably taken the liberty of talking to our cook behind my back? She told the same story to Emily's aunt when she came looking for her — the same lady who I assume has reported her as missing. But to be perfectly candid with you, officer, the girl was not greatly endowed with beauty and although she had a certain dignity about her and adequate manners, I find it difficult to believe that she would have attracted any young man sufficiently for him to have accepted responsibility for her future welfare. Then again, as I have no doubt you have occasion to observe in your professional capacity, you simply can't be certain of anything with young people these days.'

'Quite so, madam,' Percy agreed. 'Did you yourself know of any young man that she might have been seeing?'

'We would have firmly prohibited anything of that sort. Given my husband's elevated professional position, we couldn't possibly have tolerated any such loose behaviour.'

'Your husband being...?' Percy enquired politely.

'Spencer Mallory, senior partner of Mallory and Grainger in The Strand. He lists members of the nobility among his clientele, so clearly we could not be seen to encourage anything that smacked of immorality.'

'Quite. Just a few more questions, if I may?'

'Why aren't you writing any of this down?'

'One of the perks of *my* profession is the development of acute powers of memory, madam. Now, if I may ask, did Miss Broome take everything she possessed when she went missing? I'm really enquiring whether or not her departure was deliberate and planned in advance, or if she simply slipped out for the evening and met with foul play.'

'Our staff members are not encouraged to "slip out for the evening", as you put it,' Mrs Mallory advised him down her nose. 'Not the ones who live in, anyway.'

'Quite. And finally, if I may — had she recently been paid? Put another way, would she have been in possession of money with which to purchase transport?'

'She was paid monthly and would therefore have recently been in possession of almost seven pounds, plus whatever she may have saved up, of course. There's a railway station on Hampstead Road, as you presumably know, and from there one can travel all the way into the East End, from where I believe she originated. I suggest that you ask there if you wish any further information regarding her current whereabouts.'

This was one of the politest invitations to leave Percy had received in recent months and he opted to take the hint. As the same maid opened the front door for him and handed him his bowler, she smiled and said, 'I hope you find them.'

It wasn't until he was halfway back down Heath Street on his way to the railway station that it occurred to Percy to wonder what the girl had meant by *them*.

Chapter Four

Percy strode through the front entrance to Bethnal Green Police Station under the familiar glare of the desk sergeant.

'You again,' the sergeant observed unnecessarily. 'Inspector Mitchell's in a foul old mood this mornin', so don't say I didn't warn yer.'

'Has he rented out my office yet?'

The sergeant shook his head. 'No, but there's two sergeants from our lot waitin' ter gerrit back. Yer gonna be 'ere fer much longer?'

'Depends how much co-operation I get from the local force, doesn't it?' Percy smiled back sarcastically. 'Up to now it's been a few degrees short of bugger-all.'

'Then yer won't mind makin' yer own tea, will yer?' the sergeant responded gruffly.

'At least that way I'll be certain that nobody from this station's poisoned it,' Percy muttered back as he reached the staircase and took the flights two steps at a time.

It wasn't just the usual turf war between a local station and their perceived overlords at Scotland Yard. Most inner-city station personnel had long since accepted that when it came to organised crime, repeat or multiple serious offences, matters of a political nature, or crime outbreaks that were beyond their own already stretched resources, the Yard had a vital role to play in the overall policing of Metropolitan London. But just occasionally it got personal, as in this case, in which it was being implied — and certainly inferred — that Bethnal Green detectives were incapable of solving a handful of murders right under their noses.

But it went far beyond that, as the mandarins of the Yard were well aware, due to their regular liaison with officials of the recently created London County Council, which had taken over the responsibilities and functions of the now defunct Metropolitan Board of Works. A Royal Commission had reported adversely on the state of working-class housing in various parts of the nation and had been particularly critical of the position in London's East End. This had led to an Act of Parliament that empowered the LCC, as it was usually known for convenience and brevity, to acquire land, knock down slum housing and replace it with suitable accommodation for the honest worker.

It was a policy that rang with optimism through the halls of government, but had been reduced to a dull thud upon any attempt to convert it into action, particularly in Bethnal Green and the area within it known euphemistically as 'The Old Nichol'. Its narrow network of twenty overcrowded alleyways housed a staggering six thousand people in little over seven hundred cramped, damp, decrepit, vermin-ridden, insanitary hovels which, when subjected to a simple calculation, revealed an average of slightly over eight persons per house, many of which consisted of only one room measuring eight feet square.

One inevitable consequence of this sort of squalor, hitherto associated solely with some of Her Majesty's more far-flung outposts of the Empire, such as Calcutta or Bombay, was crime, and The Old Nichol hosted it in abundance. Like some of its close neighbours, counting Whitechapel and Spitalfields, it was a bottomless pit of prostitution in all its monstrous manifestations, including the exploitation of children whose ages had not yet reached double figures. It was also a vipers' nest of thieving, assault, drunkenness and disregard for authority, and if its unfortunate residents survived all of that, they were also required to surmount the endless challenge of unemployment, dire poverty and endemic disease born of insanitary and overcrowded living conditions.

One would therefore have expected the LCC to proceed with all speed in removing this blemish on the countenance of Victoria's realm and one would equally have expected those who were scheduled to be rehoused to throw up their sweaty caps in loud exclamations of joy. But this was far from the reality, and so Percy Enright had been obliged to base himself temporarily in Bethnal Green Police Station as the somewhat unwelcome implant from the new Yard headquarters on Victoria Embankment.

As soon as the word leaked out from well-placed officials inside the LCC's headquarters in Spring Gardens that there was an initiative being debated that could result in a cluster of streets in the heart of The Old Nichol being acquired for public housing, properties began changing hands and existing tenants began to be evicted. The cause was obvious — unscrupulous speculative landlords were moving in, buying up entire rows of almost totally uninhabitable residences for a pittance, ejecting the sitting tenants, then holding the LCC to ransom when it came to naming their price for the resale of the land.

None of this necessarily happened voluntarily and Percy had been called in to investigate and solve almost single-handed a spate of murders which, it was suspected, were connected with these grubby transactions. The victims were believed to have been either property owners who refused to sell, or tenants who declined to move on from the only home they knew, inadequate though it might be, to make way for new 'model lodgings' whose rents would be way beyond their capacity to pay, given the artificially inflated price that the LCC had been obliged to pay for the land.

The first demolitions were well under way by the time that the first victim — a man called Jack Broome — had been found dead under a pile of masonry in Short Street, one of the first to go under the sledgehammers. It had been believed that he had been a tragic victim of a workplace accident, given that he was a builder by trade, but then it had been reluctantly conceded, when penetrating questions were asked by LCC officials, not only that Jack Broome had not been employed in any demolitions in Short Street, but that he had lived in neighbouring Shoreditch anyway.

In fact, it got even more suspicious when Percy wheedled out of men of Broome's acquaintance in a Shoreditch pub that Broome had been approached by one of the new landlord organisations — 'Gregory Properties Incorporated' — to conduct the demolition work in question, but had blankly refused on the ground that people were still living in those houses, who had twice refused to move on. Those people had no longer been there at the time of the demolitions themselves, but one of them — a labourer called Jamie Drury, the head of a family of six — had been found face down in the Limehouse Basin of Regents Canal where he worked, ostensibly having fallen from a barge. Percy had yet to add that particular suspicious death to his list, partly because he had enough to investigate already, and partly because it was currently the subject of a demarcation dispute between 'H Division, Whitechapel' and 'Thames Division', neither of whom would accept that it fell within their remit and Percy had already ruffled enough feathers in Bethnal Green.

These had not been the only suspicious deaths of residents of Short Street. During the past few months, no fewer than five former residents of the same line of slums had been found dead, either in full view in the middle of the lane or buried under rubble. The somewhat embarrassed custodians of law and order in Bethnal Green Police Station had persuaded themselves that these were all victims of accidents when they had wandered too close to the demolition work, a fact seemingly corroborated by the fact that all of them had died from head injuries.

Those injuries could be explained away as the result of the victims being caught under the masonry when they remained stubbornly inside their condemned homes, despite several warnings to get out. But the police surgeon called in as a matter of routine to examine each corpse, while giving his official conclusion of 'accidental death from causes unknown' to the local constabulary, had sent a private message to Scotland Yard that the fatal injuries bore all the hallmarks of a swift and determined blow with a sledgehammer.

It was hardly surprising that it was now being suspected by senior Yard officials that all was not well with local policing, hence Percy's presence. Negligent and indifferent though the local force might be at best, at worst they were suspected of collaboration with the property developers. It was certainly true that the remaining families in Short Street had become noticeably more eager to vacate their squalid homes following the five deaths and Short Street itself was now a line of ominous rubble with bitter memories buried beneath piles of brick and tile. Percy was not surprised that his presence in Bethnal Green Police Station was resented and the sooner he completed his investigations, the happier all concerned would be.

Every line of enquiry that Percy had sought to pursue had ended in the same frightened denials by potential witnesses, surely terrified that they would end up in the same state as their neighbours. But one name kept cropping up in conversation just before the fear lit a dull glow behind the eyes of those he was appealing to for information. That name was 'Michael Truegood', the new local rent collector for Gregory Properties, though the collection of rent seemed, for him, to come second to his real mission, which was to advise those who were handing him their miserable handfuls of hard-won coins that they would soon be required to vacate, along with their families and belongings — or else. There was little doubt in Percy's mind that Truegood was the key to all the recent deaths and from the physical description that Percy's informants had given, he knew that Truegood was over six feet in height and built like the Shoreditch gasometer, with a fearsome black beard.

The closest that he'd come to learning of Truegood's real role in what had been happening had been courtesy of a brave young man who was so incensed by the apparent murder of his former employer, Jack Broome that he'd asked to speak to Percy in confidence. They had met in the 'The John Barleycorn' public house in neighbouring Shoreditch. His name was Tommy Dugdale, a roof tiler employed by Broome and romantically inclined towards his daughter, whose name at that time Percy had not known. Now he believed that Providence had handed him another useful card, since it was too much to put down to coincidence that Jack and Esther's upstairs neighbour Alice Bridges was seeking news of her niece Emily, whose surname was Broome, whose builder father had been murdered, and who had been romantically attached to a roof tiler named Tommy.

Tommy had himself finished up dead two days previously, perhaps as the result of meeting with Percy and advising him of his suspicions that 'Michael Truegood' was in fact the new identity of a local terror who everyone had believed to be dead. His name had been Michael Maguire at birth, but he had delighted in the nickname of 'Mangler' in the days during which — without any beard — he'd been the undisputed leader of a local team of 'enforcers' who were either available on hire, or in their spare time ran a nice line in 'insurance' for those anxious to ensure that their businesses did not suffer any unfortunate 'accidents'.

Percy had received this invaluable information a week ago and he feared that Tommy had been spotted talking to him and had paid with his life. This gave rise to the ominous suggestion that Percy's identity was known to Truegood and his bullies. There was also the possibility that Tommy's death was linked to the disappearance of Emily, either because she'd taken her own life when she learned of the death of her loved one, or because Tommy had also told her what he knew, thus making her the next target.

The trail was not yet entirely cold. Tommy had not, as all the others had, died from a sledgehammer blow. Instead, according the crime report, he'd been found up a back alley with a knife buried deep in his chest. The finding of the body had been reported by a young female called Daisy Trembelow. She was obviously the next one on Percy's interview list, although he was nervous about thereby bringing about her death by association.

Inspector Mitchell was in the process of hanging his suit jacket on the coat rack when he saw Percy lounging against his doorframe.

'I wasn't advised that you wished to see me,' he grunted with displeasure.

'That's because I didn't announce the fact,' Percy replied with a deadpan expression. 'I won't keep you long — I just need to know where I can find a local resident called Daisy Trembelow, who reported the discovery of the body of Tommy Dugdale.'

Mitchell laughed.

'We call her "Daisy the Kneetrembler", given her chosen profession. Like most of the females in this hellhole, she's a tottie and she stumbled on the body when she went up the alley with a sailor in the course of her normal employment. She alerted the first bobby she could find, no doubt leaving her mark unsatisfied, although he'd have been able to choose plenty more from the line that forms nightly on Old Nichol Street. His mother identified his body at the mortuary, after Daisy told us who she thought it was. She knew him quite well, apparently.'

'Do you have an address for Daisy?'

Mitchell smirked. 'Like 'em young, do you? She's only fourteen.'

'She's also the only one who can answer my next set of questions — or yours, for that matter.'

'What's the Yard's interest in this?' Mitchell asked.

'None at present — I'm dealing with it in a private capacity. Friend of a friend asked me to enquire about the disappearance of her niece and Tommy Dugdale was part of her past. Now I'll have to tell her that a "past" is all he's got.'

'A lady friend?'

'In a manner of speaking. But you didn't tell me where I might find Daisy Trembelow.'

'After eight in the evening, you can guarantee she'll be in the tottie queue halfway up Old Nichol Street. She looks her age and has ginger hair that's normally in need of a wash. God only knows how clean the rest of her is. Let me know if you learn anything that'll help in this case.'

The following evening, seated round the kitchen table, Percy was breaking the bad news while Alice was sniffling into her handkerchief, Esther was shaking her head sadly and Jack was all ears.

'So, what did this girl Daisy have to tell you?' Jack asked.

'She told me to do one when she learned that I wasn't a potential customer. You'll have to do instead, my girl.' Percy turned to Esther.

'I *beg* your pardon?' Esther exploded, to Jack's considerable amusement. 'Do I look like the sort of woman who'd be found on street corners?'

'I think he meant,' Jack advised her between fits of choking laughter at the sight of their two faces, Esther's all outrage and Percy's one of acute embarrassment, 'that you'll have to approach the girl instead.'

'Give me one good reason,' Esther demanded.

'Emily Broome,' Percy replied. 'Tommy Dugdale was one possible lead to where she might have gone and he was also *my* only lead to all these deaths in Hell's Kitchen.'

'Please, Esther,' Alice pleaded quietly. 'I'm *so* worried that Emily might have gone off with Tommy. She might be the next one to be murdered.'

Esther looked round despairingly at the others before responding. 'Just so that I've got this right, you want me to walk up to a line of street prostitutes in one of the most lawless areas of the East End to try to persuade a fourteen-year-old girl to tell me what she knows about the man's body she found?'

Percy grinned. 'Yes, that's what I'm suggesting.'

'Don't stand there for too long, unless you want to supplement the housekeeping money,' Jack joked. 'Compared with that raddled lot, you could probably make a quid a time.'

He managed to duck an outraged swipe aimed at his head, but Esther wasn't finished with her objections.

'How can we be sure she'll tell me anything?'

'We can't,' Percy conceded, 'but she's the only remaining lead we've got at this stage. According to what I learned in the Bethnal Green police station, she knew the boy and I'm hoping that we might get a line on who killed him and why. It *may* have been a simple street fight, or perhaps someone wanted to silence him for what he seemed to know about this Truegood character.'

'I hope I didn't bring about his death by getting you to enquire after Emily,' Alice said tearfully.

Percy hastened to reassure her. 'Don't worry about that for one moment, Alice. I'm sure it's only coincidental that he was an old flame of Emily's. But I might be able to find out if she ran back to him when she left the employment of the Mallory family. There had to be a good reason for her giving up a secure position like that; love — as they say — conquers all.'

'There must have been other witnesses to the murder of Tommy, surely?' Jack ventured uneasily.

'There's only one that I know of, at this stage,' Percy reminded them all. 'That's why we need to speak to Daisy Tremblelow, and that's why we need to enlist Esther's services.'

'At least this time I'm not being made the bait for a homicidal maniac,' Esther muttered, 'although it's high time that the Metropolitan Police began paying me for my services.'

'You may be offered payment for more personal services,' Jack teased her and this time the flat of her hand didn't miss.

Chapter Five

It was just after seven the following evening when Esther sidled up to the line of women that had begun to form in front of the bootmaker's shop that had only just closed its doors for the day. It was early summer, so still broad daylight, and the penetrating rays of the sun that was retiring for the night over the rooftops of the factories were doing the women no favours as they stood there in their bonnets and other finery, looking hopefully up and down the crowded thoroughfare for their first mark of the evening. Percy was standing discreetly in a shop doorway across the road, twisting his bowler in his hand and keeping a watchful eye out for Esther as she approached the first woman in the line, a stout lady in her early forties who shot her a disapproving frown as she took in the quality of her outdoor clothing.

'You new around 'ere, darlin'? If so, piss off somewhere else, 'cos yer'll ruin trade fer the rest've us.'

'Actually, I'm looking for Daisy,' Esther explained.

'Which one would that be, then? There's three o' them in line ternight.'

'Daisy Tremblebow?'

'Oh, *that* un. The one wi' the ginger barnet? That's 'er, three from the end. You 'ere from the buildin' people?'

'No, I just want to speak to her for a minute or two. Thank you for your assistance.'

'Think nothin' of it, lovey. Just get lost when yer've done wiv 'er.'

With an encouraging smile across the road in Percy's direction, Esther moved down the line until she reached the scrawny teenager with the tangled light ginger hair and the resigned facial expression.

'Are you Daisy Trembelow?'

'Wotsit ter you?' Daisy asked.

Esther recoiled slightly from her gin-sodden breath.

'I need a moment of your time.'

'That costs money,' Daisy advised her.

'How much do you normally charge? If I give you a quid, will you talk to my gentleman friend over the road there?'

Daisy squinted across the road to where Percy was standing with a reassuring smile.

''E's a copper, ain't 'e?'

'Yes, he is, but you're not in any trouble, I promise you. We both need to know about your friend Tommy Dugdale and how he came to die.'

'Knife through the chest is 'ow 'e come ter die,' Daisy all but spat onto the pavement. 'It were 'orrible — all that blood down 'is shirt.'

Esher judged the time to be right, as she adjusted her bonnet in the pre-arranged signal to Percy that he could cross the road. As he came closer and Daisy's eyes narrowed in suspicion, Esther reached into her handbag and extracted a gold sovereign, which she handed to Daisy with a hasty reassurance that she wasn't about to get into any trouble.

'This man's called Percy,' she advised Daisy, 'and he wants to find out as much as he can about young Tommy, that's all. Tommy's girlfriend's very upset about his death.'

'Who might thatta bin, then?' Daisy replied suspiciously. 'I didn't know 'e 'ad no girlfriend, although a good lookin' lad like 'im — well, 'e wouldn't o' needed ter choose outta *this* queue, let's put it that way.'

'He had a lady looking out for his interests,' Percy explained in his softest voice, 'and she's employed us to find out how he came to die. She's not short of money, so there's possibly some more in it for you if you can tell us what you know about him and give us any information you can about who killed him.'

Daisy looked anxiously round before answering.

"'E first come inter The Nichol a few years since, doin' a roofin' job wi' a bloke called Jack Broome an' we got proper friendly when 'e stopped ter eat 'is dinner a few doors down from us. We got talkin' an' then once 'is boss got a few more jobs from the landlord we took ter meetin' regular like. Then when the new landlord took over, it were like 'e wanted nowt more ter do wi' the place. 'E told me that things weren't quite right about the plans they 'ad fer them new 'ouses we're always 'earin' about an' that the bloke collectin' the rents were a right bad 'un. 'E gimme a name an' all, but I don't rightly remember it now.'

'Michael Maguire — or maybe "Mangler"?' Percy enquired.

Daisy nodded. 'Yeah, that were it, right enough — Mangler Maguire. I asked me Dad if 'e knew 'im an' that's when Dad told me ter stop talkin' ter Tommy, since he must be a wrong 'un if 'e knew Maguire. I tried tellin' Dad that Tommy were just tryin' ter warn me, but it made no difference. Then bronchitis got me Dad an' by then we wasn't seein' Tommy around the place any more. Then I found 'im dead, like I said.'

'The night you found his body,' Percy asked, 'did you see anyone else around?'

'No,' Daisy replied with a vigorous shake of her head. 'We went up that alley 'cos it's kinda private, yer know? We got ter the top, where that ironmonger's is an' we was just goin' ter get down ter the business when I spotted this 'eap o' clothes propped up against the wall. 'Cept it weren't no bundle o' clothes — it were Tommy, poor bastard.'

Surprising both Esther and Percy, tears began to well in Daisy's eyes and Esther reached instinctively inside her handbag and held out another sovereign, but Daisy shook her head.

'Nah, yer alright, if yer sure I won't get in no trouble? It's good ter be able ter tell someone what's interested, 'cos the coppers round 'ere couldn't care less. Just another stiff ter them.'

Percy tried to reassure her. '*They* might not have cared, but I do, Miss Trembelow, and I'll do everything I can to find the person who killed Tommy.'

'Word on the street's that it were the same team what done all the others around the same time — them what's in the pay o' the bastards what's knockin' down the 'ouses. They reckon' our street'll be the next 'un.'

'It must be very worrying for you, not knowing if your home's going to be demolished,' Esther murmured as she made another attempt to hand Daisy a gold sovereign.

Daisy spat on the ground and glared at her.

'An' what 'ome would *that* be, exactly? It's alright fer you. You an' yer fancy clothes an' posh 'at, throwin' gold coins around like Lady Bountiful! I bet yer got an' 'usband at 'ome what can always put food on the table an' cuddle yer warm on cold nights. *You* don't need a shillin' a night fer a bed in a doss'ouse. An' even if yer ain't got no 'usband, there'd be no shortage o' fancy blokes ter keep yer supplied wiv gold coins in exchange fer lettin' 'em spend theirselves between yer legs.'

'Thank you, Miss Trembelow,' Percy said quietly as he took hold of Esther's arm and steered her gently away.

'Sorry,' Esther whispered as they reached the safety of Hackney Road and left The Old Nichol behind them.

'That's alright,' Percy assured her, 'I think she told us all she knew, but it doesn't really get us any further.'

'It's a shame it wasn't of any more value,' Esther replied, 'but you still owe me a gold sovereign.'

'You mean that Alice Bridges does.' Percy smiled. 'Perhaps she can work it off with extra babysitting.'

The following evening Jack was surprised to find Percy back on his doorstep when he answered the knock on the front door.

'Always a pleasure, Uncle Percy,' Jack assured him as he opened the door, 'but I'm afraid we ate earlier.'

'So did I, at that chophouse round the corner. But I'm pretty sure the lamb was cooked in seawater, so I'd appreciate a cup of tea.'

'How's it going?' Esther asked as she poured. 'Sorry again for getting Daisy all outraged.'

'That's alright,' Percy assured her. 'From what she was able to confirm, it looks as if my initial suspicions were correct and that I'm dealing with a well organised team.' He nodded his head for the biscuit that Esther was offering him from the open tin.

'And you're no nearer to locating Alice's niece?' she enquired as she closed the tin quickly before Jack could help himself.

'Regrettably not,' he conceded.

'So, what now?' Jack asked.

'How's your leg coming along?' Percy asked.

'Pretty good, actually,' Jack replied with a broad smile. 'We went as far as Coram's Fields today and had a picnic lunch on a bench.'

'You presumably didn't walk all the way?'

'No, we took a bus,' Esther explained. 'Provided he doesn't have to go upstairs, Jack can manage getting on and off a bus platform.'

'That's good news for me, but bad news for you two, hero and wife.' Percy grinned in that irritatingly knowing way of his.

'Why's that?' Jack asked, half prepared for the answer.

'Because, dear nephew, it's time you went back to work. The holiday's over and I need you behind a desk.'

Chapter Six

After two changes of horse bus, Jack felt as if he'd already done a day's work as he reported for duty at the front desk inside the impressive building on Victoria Embankment that housed the Scotland Yard headquarters.

At least he'd stopped looking like Long John Silver and could get around, somewhat painfully and hesitantly with the aid of a walking stick. The desk sergeant sent for his supervisor, who in turn sent for the Chief Superintendent, who immediately delegated the task of what to do with Jack to an Inspector Grierson, who looked Jack up and down appraisingly.

'Can you walk up and down stairs, son?'

'Yes, Inspector,' Jack lied, since he'd been sitting in the front entrance for well over an hour and would rather attempt to run a mile down the Embankment than remain there any longer.

'That's alright, then,' the Inspector said, nodding approvingly, 'since I've been told that you've been allocated to Records, so your first task will be to get your arse up two flights and report to Sergeant Ballantyne. Off you go, peg-leg.'

If Jack was hoping that this would prove to be the one and only taunt for the day he was sadly disappointed as he was introduced to his new colleagues in a large room with far too many desks and a view out over the rear of the premises to what looked like a stable block.

'Here's the latest walking wounded,' Sergeant Ballantyne announced to those already sitting at the remaining desks. 'As yer can see,' he said to Jack, 'yer not the only one who's suffered in the service of Her Majesty.'

Jack stopped feeling sorry for himself as he looked around at the all-too-visible injuries of his fellow exiles in the land of perpetual paper. There were several with walking sticks like his own propped up precariously at the side of a desk and many others who were clearly being required to work one-handed, to judge by the slings and the Plaster of Paris casts that they were supporting. There was even one poor soul with his head and neck encased in a wire cage of some sort, which made the simple act of looking around a full-body operation.

'That's yer desk, over there.' The sergeant motioned towards a table in the corner already piled high with files, folders and assorted documents.

'We saved you a few,' said the man with the metal headframe, smiling. 'Nothing personal, but blokes come and go so fast through here that we take the opportunity of dumping the hard or boring ones onto a spare desk for the next poor sod through the door. Today, that's you, I'm afraid. I'm Tim Kilmore, by the way, and I wasn't born with this ivy latticework round my head. I copped that in an argument with a Peterman armed with a neddy. How did you come to disqualify yourself from arse-kicking contests?'

'Jack Enright,' Jack chuckled. 'I fell under a horse in Limehouse.'

'You that 'ero cove that's gonna be given a gong by Her Royal Misery?' another of them enquired.

Jack nodded reluctantly. 'So I was told, but that was over a month ago, so probably not.'

'You'll deserve a medal if you get through that lot,' Tim grinned with a nod at the pile on Jack's desk.

'I'd better make a start then, hadn't I?' Jack replied with a sigh as he propped his walking stick against the side of his new desk and sat down.

Two hours later he'd signed off on several 'Crime Summary' reports that involved comparing the original incident documents with the edited versions of them on the Summary and ensuring that nothing significant had been left out. The only one to vaguely excite his interest was the one from his old station, Leman Street in 'H Division, Whitechapel'. It was while stationed there that he'd first met Esther, during that now infamous series of prostitute murders and he was gratified to note that the grimy confines of his old beat had now reverted to being simply the haunt of thieves, con-men and prostitutes who only got arrested because they hadn't chosen an alley dark enough to conceal their working activities.

Given his late start, it seemed a very short working morning before colleagues began to rise from their desks, stretching and announcing the identity of the local food vendor who was being graced with their custom that day. Jack had come armed with sandwiches filled with the leftovers of yesterday's Sunday roast and as he sat munching them happily in the tearoom at the end of the corridor, he reminded himself that Uncle Percy had a particular reason for wanting him back at work and he sent for the criminal history of Michael Maguire.

Or, as it turned out, most likely the criminal history of the *late* Michael Maguire, since the previous year the man in question had been sentenced to death for murder. Jack tutted in exasperation as he rose and walked down the long hallway back to the Records front desk, or the 'sweetie counter' as his new-found colleagues had dubbed it. He consulted the brief note he'd scribbled on some scrap paper back at his desk and enquired, 'How soon after an execution do we get the hanging records from Newgate?'

'It varies,' came the less than helpful reply. 'Who are you after?'

'Michael Maguire, Newgate, 6th March last year.'

Eventually the man on the desk came back into view holding a small file, for which Jack was required to sign before he was able to take it back to his desk, by which time his healing leg was calling for a rest from all the walking and standing.

Jack felt slightly nauseous as he read the detailed record of Maguire's final few days in the condemned cell, where he'd been weighed and measured for height. At slightly over six feet in height and weighing one hundred and ninety-two pounds he must have been a fearsome sight, even without the heavy facial scarring that completed the description.

A quick look at the accompanying crime report described how he'd acquired those scars; burn marks from a botched attempt to torch a canal-side warehouse whose proprietor had declined to pay for the necessary fire insurance. A nightwatchman had died in the course of attempting to douse the flames, but Maguire had copped a blazing face full of whatever liquid he'd been handling to start the fire. Given the innocent man's death, Maguire and a co-offender called Charles Grieves, who'd been unwise enough to remain in order to extinguish Maguire, had been found guilty of murder and sentenced to hang. Their executions had been set for the same day, Monday the sixth of March, a "hanging day" on the jail's calendar.

Back to hangman James Berry's completed report and a bit of a disappointment in the sense that only one of them had hanged that day. But at least it was Maguire, according to the detailed record. Then Jack was pulled up with a start.

The man who'd been 'launched into eternity' had received a fairly lengthy drop of around six feet, calculated to end his life instantly and deliberately on the long side since he'd only weighed one hundred and forty-five pounds. Even allowing for prison food, Maguire had lost a lot of weight during his time in the condemned cell. Still, Jack reasoned, it was guaranteed to stunt your appetite, sitting there waiting for the dreaded day. But could that also account for the fact that the man on the trapdoor had been only five feet seven in height?

Almost certainly, the man recorded as dead an hour or so later (*Dear God, did it take him that long to die?*) had not been Michael Maguire, although according to the prison record it had been. And why had Charles Grieves not been hanged at the same time?

Jack had two choices. He could either call for more Newgate records, thereby incurring another long wait, or he could go down to Newgate himself and examine what they had available, which meant being absent from his desk for half a day and a somewhat lengthy bus ride. Then he remembered the huge leg of lamb that Esther had bought only the other day and sent a wire to Uncle Percy down in Bethnal Green.

'I don't believe for one moment that Jack's motivation was to give you a pleasant evening off from your many enquiries,' Esther advised Percy as she tipped a handful of salt into the pan of potatoes on the stove, 'so let's get the case discussions out of the way now, over a glass of that wine that you kindly brought with you.'

'Just like old times,' Percy reflected as he pulled the cork. 'I was often round here with a bottle of wine in the early days of your marriage.'

'Usually as a bribe,' Esther grimaced. 'I hope that you and Jack aren't planning to involve me in another of your cases. The last one was the *last* one, as I told you at the time.'

'Relax,' Jack said, smiling. 'I really *do* want to give Uncle Percy a pleasant evening off from all that he's dealing with down in Hell's Kitchen, but I also need his advice.'

'Fire away,' Percy invited him and Jack gave him the full chapter and verse on the suspicious circumstances of Michael Maguire's alleged hanging.

'Do they *really* go into all that detail?' Esher shuddered. 'It's so — so *callous* and unfeeling. Just like they were weighing cattle in an abattoir!'

'Believe me, it's an improvement on the previous practices,' Percy assured her. 'At least this way they can guarantee a quick death.'

'Can we change the subject?' Esther pleaded.

'Not entirely,' Jack insisted. 'It clearly wasn't Maguire who took the drop and I wouldn't be surprised if the executed man turned out to be his partner in crime Charles Grieves. But there's no record of a second hanging, so what exactly went on?'

'Even more importantly,' Percy observed, 'where's Maguire now, if he didn't hang?'

'He should be easy to identify,' Jack pointed out, 'with those burn scars down his face.'

'Unless he disguised them in some way when he got out of jail,' Percy mused. 'Maybe grew a beard or something. And I know just such a man, who answers the general description of "He who escaped the gallows". Either that or his ghost has taken to collecting rents in Bethnal Green.'

'Let's just hope that the price of his freedom wasn't to silence poor Emily Broome.'

Percy nodded. 'I think a visit to Newgate's in order. But leave that to me — I'll probably enjoy it more than feeling like a condemned man every time I walk through the door of

Bethnal Green Police Station. In the meantime, I need all you can get on "Gregory Properties". We can meet up again when you've got them; wire me down at Bethnal Green and hopefully we can sample that new eating place across the road from the Yard.'

Chapter Seven

'Which one of you's Constable Enright?' the young boy from the Records Office asked as he stood in the doorway with a thin file under his arm.

'Over here,' Jack instructed him, as he extracted a shilling from his trouser pocket and handed it to the boy when he placed the file on Jack's desk. 'Do you do returns as well as deliveries?'

'I does fer a shillin',' the boy replied with a grin.

Jack pointed to the stack on the outer edge of his desk.

'This pile of Crime Summary reports needs to go back to the Sergeant. Are you by any chance hoping to become a police officer yourself one day?'

'Sure am.'

'Well, here's a little careers advice,' Jack replied, grinning. 'One — grow another four inches. Two — don't take bribes, even from other police officers.'

The boy went out with a cheerful whistle and Tim Kilmore tutted from the adjoining desk.

'He'll expect that every time now, thanks to you.'

'Only from me and it's better than a long walk down the hall. You should try doing it with a busted leg and a walking stick.'

'Ever tried eating through a wire cage?' Tim retorted bitterly.

Jack let the matter drop and concentrated on the recently delivered file. It was the company records for 'Gregory Properties Ltd', part of the compendious archive of company registration documents held by the Yard for use by those investigating the countless frauds being perpetrated across the nation during England's unrivalled industrial prosperity and world trade dominance. The Memorandum of Association listed its two founding members, who were also its majority shareholders and directors. The names were not familiar to Jack, so he made a note of them, before copying out its Objectives, exclusively the 'provision and erection of housing tenements to alleviate the suffering of the poor in selected areas of the County of London.' Its annual report meant nothing to Jack other than columns of figures, although its latest annual report — the one for the previous year — contained an assurance that once the company completed its current acquisition and demolition programme and began to sell back the land it had recently purchased, it would no longer be in such heavy debt to the bank.

Jack looked up in some alarm as Sergeant Ballantyne entered the busy office and headed straight for him with a solemn expression on his face.

'I've just bin told that yer've taken it upon yerself ter order files what wasn't allocated ter you in the first place. But accordin' ter my list, yer overdue at least thirty Crime Summary reports and I want 'em by four o'clock, ter give me time ter sign off on 'em afore I goes 'ome. And if I don't get 'em by then, yer'll be goin' 'ome fer the final time from 'ere. Understood?'

'Yes, Sergeant,' Jack confirmed as he lowered his head down over his desk.

Sergeant Ballantyne looked round the room with a satisfied smirk.

'An' that goes fer the rest o' you lot in 'ere. Yer may all've bin injured in the course o' duty, but this is the Scotland Yard Central Records Office, not Victoria bleedin' Park. Get yer 'eads down an' yer arses up!'

'How was your day?' Esther asked eagerly as Jack let himself through the front door to find her waiting with a smile and a welcome home kiss. 'I hope it wasn't too tiring or painful.'

'Neither,' he replied, 'just boring. It's always the same in Records and I'll go slowly insane if I have to stay in there for more than a month, even if I *am* able to run some sort of courier service for Uncle Percy while I'm in there. But they haven't kept the promise about promotion to Sergeant. Not yet anyway.'

Esther's eyes twinkled with excitement as she pointed to the hall stand.

'Looks like they kept the other promise, though. There's a letter addressed to you with "Buckingham Palace" written on the envelope.'

Percy hammered on the Newgate front gate knocker wearing the facial expression of a Grim Reaper and demanded to speak to the Keeper.

'He's having tea in his private rooms at the moment,' the Senior Turnkey advised Percy once he had been through various admission processes and several sets of gates.

'I don't care if he's having a baby in there,' Percy growled back. 'This is a matter of the utmost gravity, but if the organ grinder's not available, I'll speak to his monkey instead. Now.'

The Deputy Keeper was advised that a very irate and forceful gentleman from Scotland Yard awaited his displeasure and Percy was invited to take a seat in front of a desk the size of a shop counter, but minus any papers or other indications of work that might be in progress.

'I'm Edmund Tillotson — what can I do for you?'

'You can confirm that on the sixth of March last year — that is, 1893 — you hanged a man named Michael Maguire. You can then explain what happened to his co-accused Charles Grieves, who was scheduled to hang on the same day.'

'Surely you've consulted our records?'

'Of course I have, or rather one of my men has. The 'drop' weight for the man hanged under the name of Maguire doesn't match Maguire's physical description.'

'They *do* vary a little from the date when they're first weighed,' Tillotson advised him.

Percy's face set even harder.

'I'm well aware of that, my friend. But in my experience and contrary to what people might think, prisoners in condemned cells tend to put *on* weight. So how did Mr Maguire manage to lose forty-seven pounds in less than a week, not to mention five inches in height?'

'I've no idea, obviously. Perhaps we should speak to Mr Barrington — he's the turnkey in charge of the Condemned Suite.'

'Yes, perhaps we should,' Percy replied acidly. 'And could you also ask him to bring the prison record for Charles Grieves, who should have hanged alongside Maguire?'

'I can save you the trouble on that one,' Tillotson smiled reassuringly, but rather too glibly, Percy thought. 'Grieves was a suicide.'

'Perhaps, while we're waiting for Mr Barrington, you might explain why someone who's scheduled to hang anyway would want to commit suicide. And for that matter how he managed it, given that he was presumably under continuous watch, as is required by regulation.'

'Certainly. I'll just send for Barrington.'

'Along with the jail records for Grieves,' Percy prompted him.

John Barrington appeared after a delay so short that one could have suspected him of lurking outside in the corridor. He had a small folder in his hand, which Percy took from him after they'd been introduced and Barrington had taken the other seat in front of Tillotson's desk.

Percy ran his eyes over the contents of the folder, then looked up accusingly at Barrington.

'Not exactly your finest moment, was it?'

'Meanin'?'

'Meaning that you had a man on suicide watch, allegedly being supervised from dawn till dusk, who succeeded in committing suicide.'

'Unfortunate, certainly.'

'Dereliction of duty, certainly!' Percy thundered back, but Barrington appeared unmoved. 'How did it happen?'

Barrington shrugged.

'We was under-staffed as usual an' one o' the men went fer a leak while the other were called to the other cell, where a bloke called Maguire were goin' off 'is nut an' 'ad ter be restrained wi' ropes. While there were nobody in Grieves's cell — an' it were only fer a minute or so — 'e slit 'is throat wi' a bit of metal sewn inter 'is trousers. It musta bin there fer a while.'

'Are these men not searched at regular intervals?' Percy demanded.

'Like I said, we're under-staffed in the Condemned Suite, 'cos nobody likes the duty an' they 'as this 'abit o' claimin' sickness when they're put on it.'

'I presume that nobody was called in to certify Grieves's death? The Jail Surgeon, for example?' Percy asked resignedly.

'That's only for the ones who are hanged,' Tillotson advised him. 'That's regulation, of course.'

'And Grieves's body, as if I didn't know already?'

'In the communal grave, in a lime filled coffin,' Tillotson confirmed.

Percy glared down at the prison record, the copy of which Jack had already supplied to Percy. The original record confirmed what Percy already knew.

'The man who was hanged on the sixth of March 1893 weighed one hundred and forty-five pounds and was five feet seven. That matches almost exactly the admission details for Grieves. Did you hang a dead body?'

'The man hanged that day was a Michael Maguire,' Barrington insisted.

Percy snorted.

'I suggest that the man hanged that day was Charles Grieves, as scheduled,' Percy insisted. 'He didn't commit suicide at all — as your own records confirm, completed, no doubt, by someone who couldn't be either bribed or threatened and who wrote it down the way it was. Look at your own figures, man! They describe Grieves perfectly!'

'Then what happened to Maguire?' Barrington challenged him.

'You're not surely insisting that he's still in here, having somehow dodged the gallows?' Tillotson enquired, seemingly unmoved by what was being suggested and the utter corruption of his own men that was being revealed.

'Of course not!' Percy yelled. 'Do I look that stupid? He was sneaked out of here, wasn't he?'

'London's a big place.' Tillotson smiled unctuously. 'You'll have a difficult job justifying your unfounded allegations.'

'Take that fat smirk off your face,' Percy snarled as he stood up to leave. 'I know *exactly* where to find Mr Maguire and when I do you two will finish up in the Poorhouse. No job, no pension, no good character. Even better, you might even finish up chained to the wall in the very place where you once used to strut around like gods, until greed got the better of you. I'll see myself out.'

'I'm not so sure I'm all that hungry, but I seem to recall that fish and chips went down well on the previous occasions when I brought them in from Farringdon Market,' Percy said as he handed the warm package to Esther and the bottle to Jack. 'Hurry up and open this bloody thing — I need a drink or three after my frustrating afternoon down in Newgate.'

'I'll put these in the oven to warm up a bit more, while you two boys talk business,' Esther offered, 'but keep it quiet, because Bertie's only just gone to sleep.'

'So how did it go?' Jack asked.

'Exactly as we thought. Michael Maguire's almost certainly doing dirty deeds for the builders and demolishers who're flattening The Old Nichol, while his partner Grieves took the drop in his name. If nothing else comes of all this, Newgate will soon be looking for a new Deputy Keeper. And the way I feel at the moment, I might apply for the job myself.'

'I looked at those company records, by the way,' Jack advised him as he reached into his jacket pocket, 'although they didn't mean a great deal to me.'

'Show me anyway,' Percy requested as he took a seat at the kitchen table and a long swig of the wine that Jack poured him as he began reading. Over the top of the wine glass his eyes widened in total surprise.

'What is it?'

'Jesus blooming Christ and all the bleeding angels!'

'Uncle Percy!' Esther protested from the drawer from which she was extracting the cutlery. 'I asked you before to keep it quiet for the sake of the children. I don't want our daughter to develop the same foul mouth as you! She can talk quite fluently now and I don't want her sounding like she grew up in Whitechapel!'

'Sorry my dear,' Percy explained, 'but guess who's one of the two directors and principal shareholders of Gregory Properties?'

'One of those names was vaguely familiar, certainly. "Mallory", wasn't it?' Jack replied.

'Spencer Gregory Mallory, no less. The middle name was the one he chose for his company, no doubt intent on keeping his true identity secret from everyone except those with access to company records. But think — *why* was that name familiar to you?'

'I've been racking my brains ever since I read it,' Jack admitted, 'but it still eludes me.'

'Wasn't that the name of the man who employed Emily?' Esther said as she leaned across the table to place the sauce bottles in its centre.

'The very same!' Percy confirmed. 'You have a better memory than the man you married who calls himself a police officer, my dear. I don't suppose the other name means anything to you either?'

'Victor Bradley?' Jack asked. 'No — should it?'

'Take my advice and stay out of the Fraud Branch when you're back on two legs,' Percy smirked. 'He's an Assistant Leader of the London County Council and I'll bet Bermondsey to a brick that he's in some position of influence over the land acquisitions down at The Old Nichol.'

'Ah, got it now,' Jack replied. 'Civic corruption, you mean?'

Percy smiled broadly at Esther, who was lowering a plate of haddock and chips onto the table in front of him. 'The loud clang you just heard, Esther my dear, was the noise of a penny dropping inside your husband's head.'

'So, what do you propose to do?' Jack asked as Percy raised his knife and fork.

'Satisfy the raging appetite that just returned. *Bon appétit*, everyone.'

Chapter Eight

'Here's a toast to Jackson,' Constance Enright announced as she raised her glass high in the air. 'This doesn't mean that I approve for one second of the irresponsibility of my late husband's brother in encouraging my only son to risk his life and financial prospects in a police career. But, being an Enright, he proved himself the best at what he eventually chose to do, although I'll never understand why. So, I give you "Jackson Enright".'

As the glasses of champagne rose in unison and his name was quietly repeated by his proud immediate family members, Jack smiled back with some embarrassment and reflected on the eventful morning behind them.

First the cab ride into Buckingham Palace, with Esther sitting proudly alongside him and his mother squeezed in on his other side, as the hansom swept through the front gates. Then the shuffling and queue formation supervised by some flunkey in coat tails in the ballroom, followed by a long wait until a bustling movement in the doorway proved to be the entrance of Her Majesty herself, accompanied by a senior naval officer in full dress uniform who looked as if he'd just escaped off stage from one of the Gilbert and Sullivan operettas that were currently playing to packed houses down the road at the Savoy Theatre.

As he stood in line, Jack felt like an imposter as he listened to the naval type advising the Queen of the actions that had led to those in the line ahead of him being nominated for their awards. A Welsh coalminer who'd re-entered a caved-in seam half a mile underground in order to rescue five of his workmates; a nurse in Leeds who'd crawled into a collapsed building to administer morphine to someone trapped under a roof beam; and a fireman who'd risked being blown to pieces when he continued hosing, at close quarters, an inferno in an ammunition dump in Colchester that threatened to destroy neighbouring houses if it went up. By comparison, stopping a runaway horse seemed like a routine daily chore.

Of the Queen herself, Jack had only two memories. The first was that she was as wide as she was tall, a detail usually obscured from the general public by the fact that they only ever saw her seated, either in her processional carriage or in the traditional photographs of her with her sons and daughters during the summer months at Osborne House, ready for circulation to the newspapers in time for their Christmas editions. His second memory was that she smelled faintly of mothballs.

'Police Constable Jackson Enright, Ma'am,' the equerry had advised her when his turn came. 'Saved two young children from a bolting horse in Limehouse.'

'Why was the horse bolting, young man?' the Queen asked.

'Someone had let off a fire cracker, your Majesty.'

'Yes, quite. Skittish things, horses, as my dear late husband Albert once had occasion to learn to his cost. Well done, young man. You're too tall for me to pin this thing on you, so my equerry will do the honours. Who's next, Admiral?'

A quick pose in the Palace gardens for a police photographer who'd been commissioned to preserve the proud moment for the benefit of the *Police Gazette*, then off to the splendid lunch hosted by a very proud mother in a private room in a very exclusive restaurant in nearby Knightsbridge. The beefsteak was excellent and the celebratory cake baked by a leading *boulanger* recommended by Jack's sister Lucy melted in the mouth so easily that everyone was into their second helping before Constance remembered the toast.

'What's your next move?' Jack asked in little more than a whisper to Percy, seated to Jack's right as he occupied pride of place at the other end of the table from his mother, with Esther on his left, Lucy's husband Edward next to Percy and Lucy seated alongside Esther.

'I'm not sure which of them to tackle first,' Percy admitted. 'The obvious one's Victor Bradley and allegations of civic corruption. He was ideally placed to award the contract to Mallory's company and I need to find out if that contract came before or after Mallory started buying up properties in The Old Nichol. If it came afterwards, then clearly Mallory knew in advance where the contract would be awarded and Bradley clearly had a financial motive for awarding it to a company of which he's a leading shareholder and director. That's probably enough in itself to get him put away for a long stretch, given what is called in polite circles his "conflict of interests" in the award of Council contracts. But I haven't forgotten the other matter involving Mallory — the missing Emily Broome. I don't want to get too far up his nose until I'm satisfied that he can no longer help in our enquiries regarding the girl's disappearance.'

'That's quite enough of that work nonsense,' Constance boomed down the table. 'This is meant to be a momentous family occasion, not another opportunity for Percy to lead Jack astray.'

'I quite agree, Mother,' Lucy chimed in, still not having quite forgiven her Uncle Percy for persuading her to play the role of a ghost during a dreadful investigation in a remote part of Wiltshire the previous year, which had gone horribly wrong when a man finished up under a coal train. Lucy preferred her comfortable life as the wife of a successful Holborn architect, a mother of three and a much lauded amateur Thespian in a local theatre group. Whenever Uncle Percy was around, family members tended to get themselves recruited into unofficial roles with Scotland Yard and it was presumably only a matter of time before Constance became his next dupe.

'At least you should now think about forgiving Uncle Percy for getting me into the Met,' Jack said to his mother. 'We now have a bravery award recipient in the family and I doubt that I'd have earned that as the insurance broker that you wanted me to become.'

'At least in that profession you wouldn't have fallen under a horse,' his mother countered and it fell embarrassingly silent until Esher kicked the conversation into life by enquiring as to the health of Lucy's children. Percy took advantage of the renewed noise cover to whisper hoarsely to Jack, 'I'll come up and talk to you as soon as I have more to report.'

Chapter Nine

'There's no doubt about her identity, I suppose?' Percy said glumly as he gazed down at the naked corpse of the latest apparent murder victim on the mortuary table.

Dr Bebbington shrugged his shoulders in a non-committal gesture.

'You're the detective — I only certify cause of death and from the state of what's left of her head I wouldn't have needed a medical degree to do that. A sledgehammer or something similar, just like the others, no doubt so as to obliterate her appearance to conceal her identity. But as for that, they either got very careless, or it's a subtle attempt to confuse things. Her handbag finished up a few feet away in the rubble and it contained pawn tickets in her name.'

So far as he was being led to believe, Percy's search for Emily Broome was over. But even if he accepted, from the handbag evidence, that she was now dead, there were many other questions he'd like answered. First of all, how and why had she finished up in Bethnal Green, when her life until she became a governess in the employment of the Mallory family had been led in neighbouring Shoreditch? Had she been living right under his nose in the two weeks or so that he'd been looking for her, or had someone left the body under the builder's rubble of Short Street to make her look just like one of the others?

Where had she been most recently? Certainly not with Tommy Dugdale, given that his death had occurred a week before hers. But had she run back to him, only to witness his murder and been silenced because of what she knew of his death? Was her death completely unconnected with her disappearance from Hampstead, or had she been done away with for some reason connected with that?

The experienced investigator inside him began considering other possible motives for her death and he asked the obvious question of the police surgeon.

'Any signs of sexual assault?'

'None whatsoever,' he was assured. 'In fact, for a girl in her early twenties in this area she was quite remarkable in still being a virgin.'

That ruled out one obvious reason for her departure from her employment; she obviously had not been subjected to the usual experience of many 'live in' female domestic staff at the hands of 'the master of the house'. At least, not to the extent of losing her virginity.

'I take it you didn't know the girl well enough to be able to make a formal identification?' Dr Bebbington cut into Percy's train of thought.

'We'd never met and the only reason I'm here's because she's connected with the slum clearances,' Percy replied, opting not to reveal his additional interest.

'From a public health perspective, the sooner these infested hovels hit the ground the better,' the doctor observed, 'but you're right about the curious series of deaths. They can't all be accidents or coincidence and they've kept me from my normal work. However, my reason for enquiring as to whether or not you knew her is that the coroner will require formal identification from someone.'

Percy nodded down at the mangled facial features and shuddered at the prospect of requiring Alice Bridges to conduct any formal identification.

'That's going to be very difficult, obviously. Is there nothing else that might assist in confirming who she was?'

'There's this, I suppose,' the doctor suggested as he moved down the table and pointed to the left ankle. 'At some stage in the past — possibly during her early teens — she broke her ankle. It healed rather imperfectly, although some effort was made to set it, probably by some overworked doctor in an overcrowded admissions ward. However, this young lady probably ignored the advice which went with that setting, namely to rest it for a month or two and probably walked with a limp. Does that help?'

'Probably not, but if I can find someone who once knew a girl called Emily Broome who walked with a limp as a teenager, would the coroner accept that?'

'He'd probably have to, in the circumstances. I've experienced less satisfactory identifications during my extensive career as a police surgeon and the coroner's jury would probably accept his direction to bring in a verdict regarding "a female believed to be" whatever her name was.'

'Emily Broome,' Percy reminded him gloomily. 'If it is her, she maintained a family tradition. Her father went the same way when he crossed the wrong people. And that may have been Emily's final mistake.'

Percy walked sadly back to Bethnal Green Police Station to check the business address of Mallory and Grainger, solicitors, in The Strand. He wasn't in the mood for another interview with that dreadful Millicent Mallory in her well-appointed lair in leafy Hampstead and in any case he had another matter to take up with Emily's previous employer. He might even require *him* to perform the identification. The prospect brought a thin smile to his lips as he hopped onto the bus at Shoreditch and asked its conductor which changes of route would enable him to get to where the other half of London's starkly contrasted population lived and worked.

'Of *course* I don't have an appointment,' Percy grumbled in reply to the standard 'go away' question posed by the somewhat imperious lady behind the reception desk in the front entrance to the intimidating suite of rooms across the road from the Law Courts. 'We gentlemen of the Yard rely upon being unexpected.'

'He has someone with him at present, but if you'd care to take a seat over there...'

It was as much a command as an enquiry and Percy took a seat on one of the leather chairs and reached for one of the brochures on the coffee table in the centre that advertised the firm's many services to the no doubt well-heeled clientele they were hoping to attract. Since commercial property investment, corporation formations and family trusts weren't quite in his league, Percy was about to count the number of pieces of crystal in the hanging chandelier in the foyer when the door opened from inside the capacious office overlooking the crowded thoroughfare and a large man dressed in immaculate, if somewhat gaudy, chequered tweeds emerged, being ushered out by a tall grey haired man whose air of distinguished authority left little doubt that he was Spencer Mallory.

'I'll have the deed drafted and ready for signature within a week,' Mallory assured the gentleman who was presumably his client. He turned in the act of retreating back behind the polished cedar door, before being interrupted by the Gorgon from the front desk.

'There's a gentleman to see you, Mr Mallory,' she called out, adding, 'He says he's from Scotland Yard.'

'Principally because he is,' Percy advised them both, in case he was being mistaken for an imposter. 'May I trouble you for a moment of your no doubt very expensive time, Mr Mallory?'

Mallory frowned for a moment before remembering his manners and reinstalling his genial facade, as he indicated with a generous sweep of his arm that Percy was welcome to enter his office.

Having taken the seat indicated among the cluster of leather casual chairs that surrounded another coffee table and having declined the offer of coffee, Percy employed the tried and tested tactic of a silent stare, but it clearly wasn't working this time.

'I don't do criminal matters, Mr...?'

'Enright. Detective Sergeant Enright.'

'Quite. As I say, I don't do criminal matters, so how can I help you?'

'You employ criminals, though, and that's why I'm here,' Percy advised him with his 'I'm enjoying this' smile.

'I beg your pardon?'

'Michael Truegood. You employ him, I believe, in connection with your property interests in Bethnal Green. As a rent collector.'

'I leave the details to others,' Mallory assured him. 'The person in charge of the Bethnal Green project is a Mr Arthur Daniels and he has a site office in Little Nichol Street.'

'So you're not able to tell me whether anyone took up, or indeed requested, any references for Mr Truegood before employing him as a rent collector?'

'Of course not, as I said. Why, is he in trouble?'

'He should be dead, Mr Mallory. Not to put too fine a point on it, he should have been hanged over a year ago. For murder. He's working under the assumed name of "Truegood" following his escape from Newgate Prison and his real name is "Michael Maguire". Although to those in mortal fear of him he's also known as "Mangler".'

'Most unfortunate, obviously and I'll have Mr Daniels check that out without delay, but as I've already advised you, I leave the detailed day-to-day affairs in Bethnal Green to others.'

'Did you employ Emily Broome, or did you leave that to your wife?' Percy fired without warning, looking for some reaction on the self-assured countenance in front of him.

'Emily Broome? The girl who went missing? Have you found her?'

'In a manner of speaking. Her body finished up on your demolition site in Short Street. That's in Bethnal Green, in case you leave matters of street geography to others as well.'

Mallory's face had lost a great deal of its colour as he stood up, walked to a sideboard, poured himself a large whisky and came back to his seat after Percy declined his gestured offer to pour him one as well.

'She's dead, you say?'

'Correct. Almost certainly murdered, unless she was unwise enough to step voluntarily in front of a swinging sledgehammer.'

Mallory looked across at him almost in supplication.

'Was there any sign of two infant children?'

'No — why?'

Mallory swallowed some more whisky before looking back up from where his eyes had been surveying the luxurious carpet and smiling in a pathetic attempt to keep it casual.

'I suppose we should have involved the police at the time, but my wife wouldn't hear of it, because of the threats. And it was also her money that was paid over. When it had been paid and there was no sign of the children, we feared the worst and by then of course it was too late to involve you people.'

Percy took out his notebook and let out a long sigh, partly for effect.

'You've already completely lost me, apart from the suggestion that there's been some sort of kidnap of two children. Perhaps you should take a few deep breaths and start at the beginning.'

'Yes, of course. Sorry. You see, when Emily went missing, she wasn't alone. She didn't simply walk out on us — she failed to come home one afternoon after taking the twins for their usual fresh air in the nearby Park. They're only eighteen months old and their names are George and William. We'd supplied Emily with a specially constructed double perambulator contraption — it looks like a sort of human wheelbarrow and it accommodated both children in such a way that Emily could simply push it along around the ponds at the Park, so that the children would get the fresh air that's so conducive to infantile development.'

'And all three of them failed to return, you say?' Percy prompted him.

Mallory swallowed hard and nodded.

'Are you sure you wouldn't like a whisky? I'm going to have another one.'

'No, thank you, Mr Mallory. Just tell me what happened when Emily failed to return from what you tell me was intended as a routine walk in the Park. We *are* talking about Hampstead Heath, I take it?'

'Yes, but most of us who live in the vicinity simply refer to it as "The Park". Anyway, when Emily first failed to make it home in time for tea, we just assumed that she'd been delayed, perhaps stopped to talk to someone, you know? Then once it started to get dark — it was late spring and so the sun didn't set until mid evening — I went looking for them, in case there'd been an accident or something.'

'But you obviously found no trace of them?'

'No, nothing. Then two days later this note was pushed through our letterbox. It must have been delivered sometime during the night, because it was lying underneath the normal mail delivery, which usually drops through the box at around seven am. It was crudely written, or at least written by someone who wished to appear semi-literate and it demanded one hundred thousand pounds for the return of the twins unharmed. It also threatened us that if we informed the police we'd never see the twins again — at least, not alive, that is.'

'That's rather a large sum of money,' Percy observed, 'so whoever was making those demands must have known that you were in a position to pay.'

'The house itself probably gives that away,' Mallory reminded him, 'but clearly we couldn't lay our hands on that amount immediately. The letter-writer obviously knew that, because he told us to leave it in a plain bag, in cash, in one of those litter disposal things at the side of the mixed bathing pond at dusk three days later. A Monday, as I recall.'

'And you did precisely as requested?'

'Yes. My wife is a beneficiary in a family trust and the trustees are myself and her two elderly uncles. The terms of the trust are such that unlimited sums can be drawn down for any purpose that might be regarded as being for the benefit of my wife or any offspring and in the circumstances we all agreed that this demand qualified. So, we went to the bank — accompanied, I might add, by two very muscular gentlemen from our demolition site in Bethnal Green — and withdrew the entire amount in cash, then left it where instructed.'

'Did you make any arrangement to keep the location under observation when the money was collected?'

'No, we were too fearful of what might happen to the children if we did. So we just waited, expecting the children to be left by the bandstand at dawn the following morning.'

'And may I assume that they weren't?'

'No, they weren't and we've been going frantic ever since.'

Percy was reminded of the cool, almost detached manner of Millicent Mallory when he'd interviewed her in connection with the disappearance of Emily Broome and wondered how any mother could remain so in control of their emotions. By that date the children would have been missing for several weeks and most mothers would have been approaching the hysterical. But now at least he understood what the maid showing him out of the house had meant when she expressed the hope that he'd find 'them'.

'Let me reassure you, Mr Mallory, that there was no suggestion that any foul play had overtaken the twins when we found the body of Emily Broome. Also rest assured that now that you've told us about the kidnapping, we'll be pulling out all the stops to find your two little boys.'

'Please do and I apologise for my somewhat haughty manner earlier. The truth is that I've endeavoured throughout my career to keep my hands clean of any involvement with criminal law, unlike some of the grubbier members of our profession. I'm relieved that we may now look to the police to find our two sons and I'm sure I speak for my wife when I say that.'

'Yes of course — she must be beside herself with worry.'

'Millicent — my wife, that is — isn't the sort to make a big display of emotion. Quite the opposite, in fact. But she was also worried about what they may have done to poor little

Emily when they took the children from her — she was very fond of them and would have put up quite a fight. But from what you tell me, her body wasn't discovered until yesterday — that's strange, don't you think?'

'I was wondering along those lines myself,' Percy advised him. 'But at least now your wife will know what happened to Emily Broome. Will she replace her, do you think?'

'Not until the twins are found. The older children are aged thirteen and eleven respectively and they're almost out of the stage of needing even a governess, given the excellent private schools that they attend. But I'm sure that Millicent will miss Emily's gift with needle and thread.'

'I beg your pardon?' Percy enquired as his brain kicked into another gear.

'Emily had considerable skill as a seamstress of sorts,' Mallory advised him. 'She always claimed to have been trained by her mother, who was employed in a local garment factory until she died — of consumption, I believe. Emily was always able to repair damaged garments and she even made matching smocks for the twins' first birthday. Such a talented girl and she'll be sorely missed.'

'I have no doubt,' Percy agreed. 'Just one more matter if I might, before I leave?'

'Certainly.'

'How long has Mr Victor Bradley been a fellow director of your property company, "Gregory Properties", as I believe it's called?'

'Since long after the Bethnal Green contract was awarded,' Mallory replied glibly.

Percy smiled. 'What made you think that date might be significant, Mr Mallory?'

'It's obvious to anyone familiar with criminal law, isn't it? The possibility of bribery and corruption allegations, which I can assure you would not be justified in this case. Victor and I have been friends since our days at Harrow and this is by no means our only joint venture together. You'll find that Victor didn't become a director of Gregory Properties until some time after we purchased the properties in Bethnal Green.'

'But, being an old friend of yours, he would have been in a position to advise you of which areas of London the LCC were seeking to renovate and where it might therefore be profitable to acquire the existing properties? That would be equally dishonest, would it not?'

'That's a totally unworthy and offensive suggestion, Sergeant.'

'I wasn't actually suggesting it,' Percy replied with a smile that was heartfelt, 'but others might.'

'In which case I'd smack them with a libel action.'

'I know as much about civil law as you claim to know about crime, Mr Mallory, but isn't it only "libel" if it's in written form? I was referring to the sort of loose talk that one hears around the Yard sometimes.'

'In which case that would constitute "slander" and I'd still respond to it with a defamation action in the High Court. "Defamation" is the collective term for *both* "libel" and "slander", just to add to your legal education.'

'Thank you, I'll bear that in mind. Has Mr Bradley been able to take more of the weight of your joint business affairs from your shoulders while you deal with the absence of your twin boys, by any chance? Only I need to know who to consult regarding the unfortunate deaths that seem to be associated with your demolition activities.'

'Victor Bradley knows nothing about the kidnapping and since I have no doubt that you'll be interviewing him with the same suspicions you obviously had about me, I'd thank you not to make any reference to it. He's not been enjoying the best of health of late and is currently taking a rest cure on his country estate in Norfolk, so he won't be available for interview.'

'Thank you for that information.' Percy smiled as he rose to leave. 'It'll save me a wasted journey to Spring Gardens. Good day to you, Mr Mallory and thank you for your assistance.'

Percy opted for a relatively long walk back via Charing Cross and down Whitehall while he got his thoughts into some logical sequence before calling in on Jack in Records. What he had hoped would assist his enquiry into one missing young lady had somehow expanded into a search for twin boys not yet two years old. And how was Emily's disappearance connected with the missing twins, if at all? Had she been held captive by the same abductors, then finally done in when her usefulness expired and if so, why wait so long? Had she been the person behind the abductions, as some sort of revenge against her employers and had it all gone horribly wrong? In either case, what had happened to the twins? Changing the options entirely, was the abduction somehow connected with the demolitions in Bethnal Green, perhaps masterminded by Mangler Maguire when he realised how much wealth his employer could produce if threatened with the deaths of his two twin boys? If Maguire was behind this, then Percy held out little hope for the current existence of the boys; the kidnap money had been paid over and whoever was holding those children had nothing to lose — and perhaps a lot to gain — by snuffing out their pathetic little lives.

Jack groaned as he saw Percy approaching his desk in Records.

'I know that look,' Jack told him, 'and I have done ever since I broke your living room window with my whip top when I was fifteen. What is it this time?'

'First of all, I want you to examine every unsolved murder report for the past two months,' Percy replied with a facial expression that excluded any possibility that this was a joke. 'Twin boys, aged approximately eighteen months, every Division of the Met and out into Middlesex and Buckinghamshire. Then check with every orphanage, hospital and church vestry in London as to whether or not, in that same period, two little boys answering that description have been abandoned.'

'Did you come armed with a thirty-six-hour day?' Jack replied sarcastically. 'And had it escaped your calculations that I already have an impossible workload? Where's the fire and why are we suddenly interested in two small boys who, I assume, have gone missing?'

'They disappeared at the same time and the same place as Emily Broome,' Percy enlightened him.

'Then the sooner you find Emily Broome, the better,' Jack countered sourly.

'I already did. She's dead.'

'Damn.'

'Quite. Fancy a cup of tea across the road?'

'Will you give me a note for Sergeant Ballantyne? He thinks I'm a slacker, thanks to you.'

'I'm going for a cup anyway. Follow me like the Pied Piper if you want a free mug of tea, possibly a cream cake and certainly the latest in the saga of Emily Broome.'

Once established at a table to the side of the bustling pavement from which visitors to London were marvelling at the public buildings of Whitehall, Percy brought Jack up to date with his latest discoveries. When he got to the bit about the need to have the body in the local mortuary that served Bethnal Green formally identified for the benefit of the coroner, Jack pulled a face.

'We can't possibly ask poor old Alice to do that. Can't I just ask her if Emily walked with a limp?'

'Give it a try,' Percy agreed. 'Now, let me tell you what I learned to my considerable consternation when I interviewed Mr Mallory.'

Listening to the additional saga of the missing twins, Jack nodded with resignation.

'Now I see the need to check on all the unidentified bodies and unsolved murders, not to mention all those places where some charitably inclined kidnapper might have left the boys so that they would be found.'

'They may be ruthless killers, remember?'

'In which case I'll be wasting my time.'

'We still need to explore every possibility, although in my gut I get the feeling that it'll lead us back to those murders in Bethnal Green. The coincidences are piling up like dirty dishes in the sink.'

'That reminds me,' Jack said, 'Esther's pushing for news about Emily and I suspect that she in turn's being pushed by Alice. How much of all this do you want me to reveal — about the two little boys, I mean?'

'Nothing yet, to Alice anyway, since it'll only upset her even more. But I haven't finished with you yet — have you still got that annual report thing from Gregory Properties?'

'Yes, why?'

'Find out when Victor Bradley became a director, then check back with the LCC on when the contract for what I believe they're now calling "The Boundary Estate" was awarded. Finally, use your initiative to discover whether Victor Bradley has a country property somewhere in Norfolk and if he's been ill lately.'

'And after tea?' Jack joked.

'After *this* tea,' Percy replied as he stood up to leave. 'I'd better show my face back in Bethnal Green and at least pretend that I'm on top of things.'

Chapter Ten

'I don't know which news is worse,' Esther said as she dabbed her eyes with her handkerchief, 'the fact that Alice's niece was murdered, or the fact that two lovely little angels have been kidnapped and possibly done away with. They'd be little younger than Bertie. Just imagine how we'd feel if it was him!'

Jack placed a consoling hand on hers as they sat at the dining table having a cup of tea.

'We have to tell Alice at some stage and Uncle Percy has a question he wants me to ask her,' he said.

Esther shuddered slightly. 'I don't think I want to be here when you have to tell her.'

'Frankly, neither do I,' Jack admitted, 'but someone has to and she's more your friend than mine.'

'Let's do it straight away, shall we? I couldn't bear sitting here knowing that we've got that awful business still to do.'

'OK, but don't mention the twins. The news is bad enough as it is.'

They finally agreed that Esther would invite Alice down for a cup of tea and that Jack would break the news. His heart in his mouth, he put on the bravest smile he could when Esther ushered Alice into the kitchen and he asked her to sit down.

'You've got news of Emily, haven't you?' she said in a voice that was trembling slightly.

'Can you tell me, first of all,' Jack requested, 'if Emily walked with a limp?'

'Yes, she did,' Alice confirmed. 'She's certainly had it for as long as I've known her, although I didn't see much of her as a child. But you said "walked", in the past tense. She's dead, isn't she?'

'I'm afraid so,' Jack confirmed as Alice's normally cheery face began to crumple in impending tears. 'I'm not allowed to give you any more details, I'm afraid, except that she finished up in Bethnal Green. That's where her body was found, earlier today.'

'That's strange,' Alice observed through watering eyes, 'because she always used to tell me that she never wanted to see even Shoreditch again and that's a class above Bethnal Green. I'm sure she can't have been living there when she — she — oh God, she was murdered, wasn't she?'

Jack nodded his head and Alice rose from the table, knocking a teacup over in the process. She rushed out of the kitchen to the front door, sobbing loudly. Esther made an attempt to follow her, but gave up and instead locked the front door and came back to join Jack at the table.

'We had to tell her, of course, and I'm glad we got it over with, but she'll probably cry for hours. I'll go upstairs and look in on her after tea. It must be awful for her, losing someone close to her like that. Imagine how that poor mother must feel about her missing twins. I'd go off my head if it were Bertie, I know I would! What can we do to help?'

'We?'

'Well, yes, I suppose I mean me as well. Presumably Uncle Percy's doing everything *he* can already.'

'Yes, and he's got me making a thousand and one enquiries.'

'Tell Uncle Percy that if there's anything I can do, he only has to ask.'

Jack smiled and gripped her hand. 'Knowing Uncle Percy, you might regret making that offer, so I won't pass it on just yet.'

Chapter Eleven

The station sergeant called out to Percy as he came back into Bethnal Green Police Station after another fruitless dinner hour in 'The Feathers', hoping to learn more about any connection between 'Mangler' Maguire and the recent spate of brutal deaths. Either nobody knew anything, or — and more likely — they did, but didn't want to end their days under a pile of builder's rubble with a face full of sledgehammer.

'A young girl come in 'ere while yer was in the boozer as usual,' the sergeant advised him with a disapproving sniff. 'Didn't want ter be seen too long in 'ere on account of 'er 'ealth, but said yer'd find 'er at this address sometime after five ternight. Said it's ter do wi' somebody called Emily Broome — ain't that the name o' the girl what was found dead the other mornin'?'

'That's her,' Percy confirmed, 'although I don't think her identity's been properly established yet. But let me see that note.'

The sergeant handed Percy his scribbled note, but neither the name nor the address rang any bells with him.

'This "Clara Manders" — is she known to police?'

'Not ter me, but she seemed a nice lass — politely spoken, an' quite well turned out, if a bit dusty. Unlikely that she's got any form, I'd say.'

'And the address — "Calvert Avenue"? May I assume that it's somewhere in The Old Nichol that's still standing?'

'Slap bang in the middle. Even *my* constables go there in twos.'

'Very well, have four of your best ready at five o'clock this evening, dressed in civvies but well supplied with billy clubs. I need to make a few arrangements before I go and meet Clara Manders.'

Shortly before five fifteen that evening Percy weaved his way through the throng of street hawkers, wagons, prostitutes, grimy workmen on their way home and children up to no good and banged on the door of number twenty-three Calvert Avenue. A stout middle-aged lady came to the door and looked him up and down suspiciously.

'Yeah?' she demanded.

'I was advised that I'd find Clara Manders here.'

'Yeah, that's right. You the copper she's expectin'?'

'That's me. Is she here?'

'Yer've 'ad a wasted journey if she ain't. Come in — an' wipe yer feet.'

'On my way in, or my way out?' Percy muttered, as he pushed past the woman and strode into the only room in the cramped hovel. In the corner stood a scared looking girl in her early twenties with what had once been a fashionable head of hair, no doubt, but was now hanging down over her forehead in need of a good brushing. The clothes she was wearing were of good quality, but now threadbare and she was barefoot.

'Miss Manders? I was told you wanted to speak to me about Emily Broome. Did you know her?'

The girl nodded, as if afraid to confirm the fact out loud, then her eyes flickered involuntary over Percy's right shoulder and instinct led him to leap sideways, just as a massive wooden club cut through the air to his side. If he hadn't jumped, it would have been his head and Percy turned quickly to confront the black-bearded giant who'd been concealed behind the door.

'Ah, Mr Maguire I presume — congratulations on your recent hanging,' Percy remarked as he took another step backwards. Maguire walked towards him with the weapon raised and as he grinned he revealed the fact that his dentist was not regularly troubled with his custom.

'Yer wasn't ready fer this, was yer?'

'It just so happens that I was,' Percy replied calmly as he reached inside his jacket pocket and withdrew a revolver. 'Between the eyes, or between the legs? It's all the same to me, but I thought you might have a preference.'

Maguire lunged forward before Percy could line the shot up and as the bullet shot harmlessly into the wall Maguire pushed Percy to the floor, then made a full body leap through the unglazed window, tangling himself in the makeshift blind as he fell out through the hole into the rear yard and scampered over a low wall into the distant laneway.

As Percy picked himself up from the floor the girl made a run for it, straight into the arms of two plain-clothes constables who had been alerted by the shot and had made short work of breaking down the inadequate front door to the mean dwelling.

'Take her in and book her for the attempted murder of a police officer,' Percy instructed them as he dusted himself down. 'And for good measure,' he added, 'invite your colleagues to do the same for the fat cow who let me in here, knowing what was waiting for me. I'll join you at the station in a short while.'

A quick snorter of whiskey in a nearby pub to calm his rattled nerves, then Percy made his way to the place where they'd taken their prizes for the evening. He grinned at the desk sergeant as he saw the fat woman being manhandled towards a cage to the side, which was the station's temporary holding cell.

'Where's the girl?' he asked.

The sergeant grinned. 'Already taken downstairs. Didn't give us no trouble — not like 'er.' He indicated with a jerk of the head towards the lady who was glaring at them both from inside the holding cage. 'She kneed Preece in the unmentionables, so I give 'er a slap round the 'ead, just so's yer know if she makes a formal complaint.'

'I suppose she's the girl's mother?'

'I ain't that posh cow's mother.'

Percy looked enquiringly at the desk sergeant, who supplied the answer.

'Martha Crabbe.'

'Well, Martha Crabbe,' Percy advised her with a grin, 'don't make any immediate plans that involve your freedom. And by the look of you, they'll only need a very short drop for you at Newgate when you go down on a capital charge. Then again, they tell me that the food in there is safe from the rats, because even they won't eat it, so you'll maybe lose quite a lot of that body weight. No extra charge. I'm going home to a nice steak and kidney supper, while you'll be lucky to get bread and lard.' He turned to the desk sergeant. 'Make sure that she doesn't get access to anything sharper than her tongue.'

He was back at the front door before Martha Crabbe gave him one more parting challenge.

'Yer won't be 'angin' either me or the girl if yer wants ter know what 'appened ter them babies!'

'Later,' Percy replied with a triumphant grin. 'Right now I have an appointment with my supper.'

While Percy had been making the acquaintance of Michael Maguire, Jack had been experiencing mixed fortunes. The morning after he'd been obliged to give Alice and Esther the bad news about Emily Broome he'd decided to purchase a newspaper to distract him from the noise and discomfort of his daily bus journey down to Whitehall, jostling and jerking through thoroughfares crowded with other horse drawn vehicles, pressed like a piece of canned meat against fellow travellers with inadequate access to a bath and with the all-pervading smell of horse dung to which the chaotic streets of the nation's capital were subject on a twenty-four basis.

Perusing the main news items on the front page, his eyes alighted on a banner headline that proudly announced the intention of the London County Council to introduce electric trams to replace the type of converted cattle wagon that Jack was currently rolling around in. Hoping that the first service might connect his home in Clerkenwell with the more salubrious and tourist filled areas such as Whitehall, he read further and learned that the announcement had been made to the gentlemen of the press the previous evening by none other than the Assistant Head of the Council with responsibility for urban planning, Victor Bradley. That was the completion of the first task set him by Uncle Percy, who he could now advise that the said Victor Bradley was not 'indisposed', but was at work and sufficiently well to be speaking to the newspapers.

However, when he asked the clerk at the 'sweetie counter' to search for any crime reports during the past few months involving the discovery of infant corpses, he was met with a sullen stare and a disbelieving demand to repeat that request. When he did so, the clerk reminded him of what he knew already.

'That's gonna take forever.'

'I know and I'm sorry,' Jack replied in a small voice, 'but it's either that or I go through them myself and I have other tasks allocated to me.'

'I'm glad that 'adn't slipped yer mind,' came a sarcastic response from behind a line of filing boxes, as the face of Sergeant Ballantyne hove into view. 'Yer still be'ind wi' all them Crime Summaries I gave yer, so what's yer interest in dead babies?'

'I'm searching the records at the request of Detective Sergeant Enright, who's investigating a series of deaths in Bethnal Green.'

'An' would that be the same Detective Sergeant Enright what's yer uncle, by any chance?' Ballantyne demanded.

'Yes,' Jack admitted weakly.

'So 'ave you an' 'im taken it upon yerselves ter open a rival police service, run as a family business?'

'Of course not, Sergeant. It's just that he happens to think that two infants may have been murdered, perhaps in Hampstead, and that their deaths are linked in some way to the deaths in Bethnal Green. And since I'm currently working in Records...'

'Not fer much longer yer not, if yer don't buck up yer ideas,' Ballantyne warned him with a sneer. 'Yer does the work what's been allocated to yer first, understand? Else yer'll be 'obblin' the streets lookin' fer other work. Understood?'

'Yes, Sergeant.'

'Right then, bugger off back ter yer desk. Yer was late comin' in and now yer at least an hour be'ind. Mebbe yer could work through yer dinner hour ter make up fer it.'

Jack threw himself angrily behind his desk and Tim Kilmore looked sympathetically across at him from inside his metal cage.

'Bad start to the day?' he asked.

Jack smiled back at him, reminded that he had nothing worth complaining about compared with Tim.

'Sort of,' he replied. 'The Sergeant thinks I'm slacking and my uncle seems to regard me as his own personal records clerk.'

'Think yourself lucky,' Tim replied. 'My uncle thinks I should be in the army. I tried to tell him that it's war out there on the streets and he just sniffed. Then when I got this metal cage he asked if I was thinking of growing tomatoes in my spare time.'

Jack chuckled and reached for the first Crime Summary on his mounting pile. An hour later a reference to a spate of recent thefts from gardens in outlying Highgate jogged something else in his memory of recent miracles demanded by Uncle Percy and he looked across at Tim.

'Any idea how to find out if a named individual has a country estate in Norfolk?'

Tim frowned. 'It's all a bit patchy, so far as I've been able to make out on the occasions when I've had to do it. I've no idea how they do things in Norfolk, but in Middlesex they've actually got a registration system, which — unhelpfully — doesn't cover any area inside the Met. Your best bet is probably to send a wire to the nearest police station to where the estate is.'

'That's the problem,' Jack grimaced, 'I don't know.'

'Better try one of the regional stations, then,' Tim advised him. 'Isn't Norwich in Norfolk?'

'No idea, but it's a start,' Jack conceded as he rose and limped back down to the Records counter, where his arrival coincided with the hasty departure of the desk clerk behind a stack of boxes.

'I know you're in there,' Jack called out with a smile, 'so you may as well come out now. You can't stay there all day.'

The clerk came back into view with a shamefaced grin.

'I thought that this time you might want a list of the Queen's dinners for the past six months.'

'Nothing that bad. I need to send a wire to Norwich. I've written the message down for you, if you'd be so good.'

Sergeant Ballantyne appeared as if from nowhere, took the note from the clerk and read it.

'And why would the location of a country estate owned by a bloke called Bradley be of interest ter you? Thinkin' of applyin' fer a job as a gamekeeper, was yer? Or is this another private job fer yer uncle?'

'I could explain if you insist, Sergeant,' Jack replied cheekily, 'but that would keep me from my desk for even longer. Here's what I've got through already this morning.'

He removed the bundle from under his arm and placed them on the counter. Ballantyne counted them quickly, then glowered back at Jack.

'Only another fifty-seven ter go, then. Don't even think about knockin' off fer dinner till I sees 'em back 'ere.'

With a deep sigh, Jack returned to his desk and made a big display of opening the pack of sandwiches Esther had sent him out with for the day and biting angrily into the first of the cheese ones as he resumed the attack on the Crime Summaries pile.

By mid-afternoon he had another fifty completed and with considerable pride he took them back to the Records desk, where they were signed off by the desk clerk.

'No luck with the dead infants yet,' the clerk advised him. 'I could do yer a dead baby in Regent's Park Lake, but we already got the mother responsible an' she's due fer trial next month.'

'No, but thank you anyway,' Jack replied glumly as he turned and limped back to his desk for what was left of his very miserable day.

The next morning promised to be even worse, as Jack approached his desk with a groan. Sitting behind it, contentedly smoking his pipe, was Uncle Percy with an enquiring look as he raised both eyebrows.

'What have you got for me?'

'You mean apart from a request for a new uncle? I'm within a hair's breadth from being sacked from the force, with your constant demands for information that I'm in no position to supply without incurring the wrath of Sergeant Ballantyne, who probably doesn't think too highly of you either, I'd imagine. He gave me a hard time yesterday and I have a horrible feeling that today will only turn out to be worse.'

'You think *you* had a bad day?' Percy snorted. 'I was attacked with a cudgel by Mangler Maguire.'

'I hope he belted some sense into your head,' Jack fired back instinctively, then remembered that Percy was not only senior in rank to him, but was also the man who had become his substitute father when his own had died when he was only fourteen.

'Sorry, Uncle, but I'm really not having a good time in here. There's nothing yet on dead babies, but I *can* advise you that Victor Bradley's back at work, if he was ever absent due to illness, that is.'

'Yes, I read the newspapers as well,' Percy replied. 'What about his estate in Norfolk?'

'I've sent a wire to Norwich, but nothing's come back yet. So, tell me about Mangler Maguire.'

As Percy recounted the events of the previous day, Jack reluctantly conceded that he was probably better off where he was, then raised a point of his own. 'If that woman reckons she knows something about the missing infants, why aren't you down there questioning her?'

'First things first. I find it very advantageous to let them stew underground before inviting them to add to my store of knowledge. By some time late this afternoon, or perhaps tomorrow, a lady who's obviously as fond of her food as Martha Crabbe will have realised that the set menu inside one of Her Majesty's lockups leaves something to be desired. In the meantime, I think a journey to Spring Gardens is in order.'

'Spring Gardens being?'

'The headquarters of the London County Council.'

'You're going to question Victor Bradley?'

'Well I'm not about to put my name forward as a Trustee on one of their School Boards.'

'Do you think he'll agree to talk to you?'

'I never met anyone yet who didn't — eventually,' Percy grinned as he relinquished his chair to Jack. 'You'd better get down to work. And keep me updated.'

'My assistant didn't tell me what this was about,' Victor Bradley complained as he gestured for Percy to take the chair on the other side of his desk.

'That's probably because I didn't tell him,' Percy replied with a polite smile. 'The sight of my police badge seemed to be sufficient.'

'So what *is* it about?'

'Gregory Properties, or more specifically, your directorship of it.'

'That was a considerable time after the creation of the Boundary Street Scheme.'

'Funnily enough, your fellow director Mr Mallory was at considerable pains to assure me of precisely that same point.' Percy smiled enigmatically. 'You're obviously both very sensitive about the possibility of being accused of corruption. So, when exactly *did* you become a director and what was your involvement prior to that?'

'Spencer Mallory and I are old school friends and we've been involved in various property developments together in the past. Mainly out in Essex, so no suggestion of bribery and corruption there. Houses along the new railway route in Brentwood and Colchester. We'd only ever collaborated as partners in joint ventures up to that point and then this Boundary Street development came up and I suggested that Spencer should consider getting involved, but that this time it might be better to form a company.'

'For you to hide behind?'

'No, in order to raise capital from shareholders. It's one of those projects where you have to outlay all the money first and make the profit once you have the resale.'

'From what I could see of your company registration documents, you don't in fact have any shareholders apart from yourselves, do you?'

'No, as it happens. We managed to muddle along with what we'd managed to raise privately and shortly we'll be selling the vacant land back to the Council.'

'At a considerable profit, no doubt?'

'An arms-length valuation of the land. There'll be no dishonest gouging, I can assure you.'

'Nevertheless, someone — either you or Mr Mallory — must have realised the potential size of the profit to be made?'

'That was Spencer, once I'd made him aware that the Scheme would be going ahead.'

'But this was something different for you two, wasn't it?' Percy queried. 'In the past you'd built houses on land you purchased for that purpose, I assume? And yet this time your interest was in property acquisition and demolition ahead of the new housing, am I correct?'

'Precisely correct. The Boundary Street construction contract will go out to closed tender in the course of the next few weeks. It will be "sealed bid" and all above board, I can assure you.'

'But Gregory Properties will be making a bid?'

'We haven't decided yet. We were due to have a Board meeting on that very subject last week, but Spencer's obviously been very distracted by this dreadful business involving the missing twins. Presumably he told you?'

'Yes, he did,' Percy confirmed, reminding himself that according to Mallory, Bradley knew nothing about it. 'But if you do go ahead, will the Council be advised that you're a director of one of the bidding companies?'

'Only if it succeeds in gaining the contract, obviously,' Bradley said reassuringly. 'We wouldn't want any suggestion that somehow I'd influenced the tender process by letting it be known that I had an interest in it. It will be strictly by price and structural proposal.'

'And will you be involved in receiving and assessing the bids?'

'Of *course* not. That would be dishonest, would it not?'

'No more dishonest than tipping off your old school friend that the Council was about to knock down half of The Old Nichol and that it would be a good time to be buying up the properties that would come up for demolition.'

'What are you suggesting, Sergeant?'

'What do you think? You seem to be quite an expert on civic corruption.'

'You're suggesting that I tipped off Spencer Mallory, using "inside" knowledge that the Council would soon be seeking to buy out the square of streets designated for the Scheme and that he should buy up all the existing properties and terminate the leases ahead of knocking down the houses to give the Council a levelled site?'

'I couldn't have expressed it better myself.' Percy smiled ominously. 'Except that you left out the bit about being awarded a directorship of the company formed for that purpose, as a reward for your use of confidential information. "Corruption followed by bribery" — it doesn't matter what order they come in, so far as I've been led to believe.'

'I paid for that directorship, fair and square!' Bradley protested, his countenance reddening in indignation, righteous or otherwise.

'Directors are appointed by shareholders, surely?' Percy countered.

Bradley nodded.

'Yes, of course. They are indeed appointed by the shareholders, but as you'll be aware, since you've obviously examined our Memorandum of Association, there are only two shareholders, myself and Spencer. What I meant was that I bought my way in by buying a fifty per cent shareholding in the company, then it was a natural progression from that for me to become a director, with Spencer as the other director, given his initial contribution of the same amount of capital.'

'And how much did each of you contribute, if I might enquire?'

'Twenty thousand.'

'So, you floated a massive operation like that, involving the purchase and demolition of dozens of tenements, on only forty thousand?'

'Yes, it was obviously a bit of a struggle, but we managed to survive by withholding certain payments.'

'Such as wages for workers?'

'Only very occasionally, but yes, unfortunately.'

'Are you aware that one of the men you employ as a rent collector — a Mr Michael Truegood — is working under an assumed name, should have been hanged for murder last year and is quite capable of organising an extortion gang if he's short of money?'

'No, of course not. I'm not directly responsible for the hiring of staff; we have a site manager for that.'

'So I was advised by Mr Mallory, but you'll forgive me if I don't quite believe that you managed to finance a project this large, simply on forty thousand pounds of initial capital.'

'Perhaps that's why you're a police officer and not a successful entrepreneur,' Bradley retorted, causing Percy to reconsider his genial approach thus far.

'How can you convince me that you and Mr Mallory haven't been using Mr Truegood — or Mr Maguire, to use his correct name — to extort additional finance out of local businesses at a very acceptable rate of interest, like none at all?'

'I don't have to convince you of anything,' Bradley replied coolly. 'Even you Scotland Yard types have to abide by the principle of "innocent until proved guilty", don't you? It's not for me to convince you of anything — it's for you to prove the opposite.'

'Indeed it is, and I'll begin with some sort of evidence of your contribution of twenty thousand pounds.'

'That'll be in the company's accounts. And I believe that you'll need some sort of warrant to obtain those from where they're normally kept.'

'Which is where, exactly?'

'In the safe behind me.'

'Then you can, should you so choose, convince me of your bona fides by producing the relevant page at this moment, so that I can convince myself that at least one part of your explanation is the truth.'

'And why should I?'

'Because if I have to call for a warrant, I'll remain here until it arrives,' Percy bluffed. 'Then I'll have access to *everything* in your safe and unless you're the most honest man in London there'll be stuff in there you most definitely don't want me to see.'

Bradley shot him a venomous look, rose from his padded chair and opened the safe with a key from his waistcoat pocket. He flicked through a bulky folder for a minute or so, then extracted a single sheet of company accounts, which he handed to Percy with what was almost a snarl.

'I'd like it back as soon as possible. Now, I assume that our meeting has concluded?'

'This meeting, certainly.' Percy smiled as he got up to leave. 'But don't make any plans to hide on your Norfolk estate or feign sickness again.'

'I haven't been sick since I was a child,' Bradley assured him, 'and I haven't been back to Horning since last Christmas.'

'Thank you again, Mr Bradley, you've been of more help than you can imagine.'

'That Manders girl wants ter speak ter yer,' the sergeant advised Percy as he re-entered Bethnal Green Police Station deep in thought.

'Amazing how a night spent staring at a wall stimulates the desire to co-operate, isn't it?' Percy smirked. 'Have her sent up to my office, but make sure that she's thoroughly searched beforehand and that the turnkey remains with her while we talk about old times.'

Ten minutes later, a very penitent Clara was led into Percy's office by a turnkey who smelt even worse than she did and Percy nodded for her to take a seat, then waited for her to take the initiative.

'You're lookin' for a girl called Emily Broome, aren't you?'

'Who told you that?'

'It doesn't matter and don't deny it, 'cos I know you are.'

'And always assuming that I am, what can you tell me about her?'

'You found 'er body in Short Street?'

'The police did, certainly. When I saw her she was on a mortuary table. Are you about to tell me how she finished up there?'

'If I tell yer what I can, will yer drop the charge against me and find me somewhere to live outside London?'

'I can certainly see to it that the charge against you is reduced from one of the attempted murder of a police officer, but I'm not a property agent. May I assume that the person you're seeking to avoid is Michael Maguire — or perhaps you know him as Michael Truegood?'

'I know 'im as Mangler and if he finds out that I did a deal wi' you, he'll have me done in, like all the others.'

'All *what* others, Miss Manders?'

The girl smiled. 'I must look more stupid than I thought. Do you wanna know about Emily Broome or not, in exchange for me not bein' done fer Attempted Murder?'

'That sounds reasonable. So, fire away.'

'She came to live wi' me a month or so ago, on the run from Mangler and 'is lot. We used to be friends when she lived in Shoreditch and we both lost our mothers at about the same time. Then when 'er dad got done in by Mangler she ran off to some place on the other side o' London, working as a nanny or something. Anyway, Mangler must have followed 'er, 'cos she told me that one day, while she was out walking wi' two little children, 'im and another bloke told her to leave them and just walk away.'

'And did she?'

'So she said. Then she went back to Shoreditch and stayed wi' her old boyfriend Tommy. Then 'e got done in one night and she was sure that Mangler was responsible, in case she'd told Tommy all about who'd taken the children. Then she reckoned that maybe 'e'd come after 'er as well, so she begged me to let her doss wi' me until she could get away, right out of London for good.'

'Did it not occur to her that if Mangler wanted her silenced, he could have done it at the same time that he took the children?'

'If it did, she didn't mention it. Anyway, she'd only been wi' me for a few nights when Mangler sent two of 'is bully boys round. We both thought we was dead, but then Mangler himself turned up and done us a deal. He said that if I was to go to that 'ouse where you found me and send for you, Emily'd have time to slip away and no questions asked.'

'Then why was Emily murdered, if you kept your part of the bargain?'

'I don't know, do I? Maybe she didn't run away fast enough, or maybe she shot her mouth off to the wrong person. Anyway, as I've explained, I was only doing what I done to save both me and Emily and I'm glad you wasn't killed.'

'So am I, funnily enough,' Percy replied, 'and no hard feelings. I'm going to be charging that awful Martha Crabbe with Attempted Murder and I'll add it to the list against Mangler when I catch up with him. And I mean "when", not "if". No reason why you should be added to the list, but it occurs to me that the safest place for you for the immediate future will be here in the police station. It'll have to be in a cell, unfortunately, but I'll say nothing about the charge against you being reduced to something much softer and then Mangler, or whoever, will have no reason to come after you. I'll leave word that you're to be fed proper meals and given the most comfortable cell we've got, but I really don't recommend that you show your face back in the street until Mangler's been buckled.'

'I won't — and thank you.'

As he watched Clara being led away, Percy let his suspicious mind wander through the events of the day. First of all to Bradley, the man who hadn't been ill when Mallory had told him that he was, presumably in the hope that Percy wouldn't go questioning him until they'd got their stories organised. The man who, according to Mallory, knew nothing about the kidnapping of the twins, but who seemingly knew all about it. Was that because he was behind the kidnappings? After all, both he and Mallory employed Maguire and it was pushing credulity too far to assume that neither man had been unaware of the man's reputation locally when they employed him to flush unwilling tenants out of The Old Nichol and add a few bodies to the rubble when voices were raised in protest.

Then the girl calling herself Clara who'd been attempting to sell him a pack of lies about Emily Broome, either of her own invention, or told to her by Emily. Why would Emily be scared of being killed by Mangler, when he'd simply let her walk away from the Park in Hampstead? And even more unlikely, if Emily had really been staying with her old love Tommy, even for a brief period before he was murdered, why was the body in the mortuary that of a virgin? And why had she been killed the day *before* this alleged deal with Mangler?

It would help the police enormously if people always told the truth, he reminded himself for the millionth time in his career. On the other hand, if they did, men like him would be out of a career and he was too old to become a jobbing gardener now.

Chapter Twelve

Jack looked up and swore with conviction. So far he'd been having a very productive morning and was almost through the new pile that the boy had dumped silently on his desk before waiting hopefully for the shilling that never came. If he kept going at this pace, Sergeant Ballantyne might even be prepared to talk to him civilly. And now here came Uncle Percy, no doubt bearing other challenges to his continued existence as a one-legged compiler of records.

'When's the next roast lamb being served up at your place?'

'And I always thought that you were a detective,' Jack muttered.

'I'm serious,' Percy replied. 'I need to speak to both you and Esther and since there's only you here, greeting me with the same enthusiasm that you would a dose of botulism, it'll have to be after hours.'

'Probably Friday. But if you're thinking of dragging Esther into this mess, let me remind you that she made a solemn vow after the last experience.'

'Vows can be broken. Ask your average nun. Can we confirm Friday?'

'I'll check with Esther. Now go away, please.'

'It's almost dinner time and the meat pies are on me.'

Ten minutes later, they were bringing each other up to date and Jack was eager to get in first.

'There's not been a report of murdered twins anywhere in the Met for the past few months — since March anyway. And Victor Bradley has a country estate in...'

'Horning,' Percy cut in with a grin.

'If you knew why did you waste my time?' Jack complained.

'I wasn't to know that the man himself would tell me, was I?'

'You've interviewed him?'

'I spoke to his verbal stone wall, certainly. And he was most insistent that his involvement with the Bethnal Green housing demolitions was a shining example of inspired business acumen rather than a nasty piece of civic corruption.'

'That's about as believable as the suggestion that the Pope's wife shops at Marshall and Snelgrove.'

'Obviously. But he seemed to be able to establish that he only became a director of Gregory Properties *after* the Council decided to flatten the centre of The Old Nichol. He bought in for twenty thousand and here's the page from the company accounts to prove it.'

Percy handed over the sheet from Bradley's safe and Jack began to examine it as Percy carried on talking regardless.

'Mind you, some things don't quite add up. Mallory was obviously anxious to prevent me speaking to Bradley when he fed me that rubbish about Bradley being absent from duty on account of sickness. And when I spoke to that girl Clara Manders in custody in Bethnal Green, it turns out that she was a friend of Emily Broome's, and Emily told her that the twins had been kidnapped by Michael Maguire. Are you listening to all this, or taking lessons in company accounting?'

Jack had been staring at the page handed to him by Percy and now he looked up with a puzzled frown.

'Remind me of how much was paid over in ransom for those twins.'

'A hundred thousand, according to Mallory. Why?'

'Probably just coincidence, but shortly after the ransom money must have been paid, Gregory Properties got an injection of exactly the same amount — one hundred thousand.'

'Give me that!' Percy demanded, read it for himself, then slapped his forehead by way of punishment. 'Thank you for that much-need refresher course on basic policing — read the *whole* bloody thing! I was so busy trying to prove that Bradley was lying that I missed something potentially more significant.'

'We don't know if it was cash,' Jack reminded him.

'They could have purchased bearer bonds or something to hide the fact that they'd suddenly had a massive cash donation. Presumably I don't have to spell out what this suggests?'

'That Mallory staged the kidnapping of his own twins in order to acquire one hundred thousand of his own money to pay it into the company's account? That doesn't make sense.'

'It does when I tell you that it wasn't his money! On his own admission, the money came from some sort of trust of which his wife was the beneficiary. The company was in deep financial trouble up until then, as you can see from the state of its balance sheet immediately before the one hundred thousand was paid in. They were in urgent need of finance and didn't want to look for more investors with whom to share this little fortune in the making, so they rigged up a fake kidnapping in order to get money from the wife's trust fund.'

'Do you think the wife was in on it?'

'Who knows? When I interviewed her in connection with Emily Broome's disappearance she didn't seem at all distracted or emotional, but then we didn't discuss the children, because I didn't know at that stage that they were missing. The good news out of all this is that those poor wee mites are probably still alive somewhere. At least, it's to be hoped that they are, given that Michael Maguire was hired to do the job, at least according to Clara Manders, who claims to have got it from

Emily herself. Did they put all the meat in your pie, by the way and sell me just the crust?'

'You sound like a man in need of a lamb roast.'

'"Lead kindly light", as the old hymn goes. Friday's tasting good already.'

'One thing I'll say for you Enright males,' Esther muttered as she removed the last of the supper things from the dining table, 'is that you lack subtlety. Percy ate his supper like it was his last, while Jack didn't eat his with the speed of light as usual, suggesting that he's nervous. Only one thing makes Jack nervous, in my experience, and that is the risk of incurring my wrath. I can safely assume, can I not, that you both want me to get involved in another of your schemes designed to get me killed?'

'Do you remember how to use needle and thread?' Percy asked with an appreciative smile.

'Why? Is there some repeat axe murderer out there whose lips you want sewn together?'

'You can begin by writing a letter.'

'To whom, and what about?'

'This time I want you to pose as a seamstress looking for private customers along the leafy lanes of Hampstead. The lady who employed Emily Broome — the mother of the missing twins — was very impressed with Emily's ability to employ needle and thread,' Percy explained. 'Her husband told me that and it was probably one of the few pieces of truth I got out of him. Now that Emily's no longer in her service, she may be in the market for a part-time seamstress, so I want you to write her a letter, making it seem like one of many that you've sent to potential customers in the high end of town. You're a young married mother of two, whose husband brings in an inadequate income, you're bored and you want to supplement the family income employing the old skills you've had to abandon since marriage.'

'At least I won't be telling any lies this time,' Esther replied acidly, 'except for the abandonment of my old skills. The scrapes that Jack gets into at work require me to convert his suits into coats of many colours, to quote from the Old Testament.'

'So, you'll do it?' Percy asked eagerly.

'Only if you tell me why,' Esther insisted.

'Ah yes, nearly forgot that bit,' Percy conceded. 'The thing is that the lady — a Mrs Millicent Mallory — didn't seem unduly distracted or bereft when I interviewed her in connection with Emily. In fact, her lack of concern ran to the extent of not even mentioning the kidnapping of her twin sons. Her husband fed me a load of lies about not wanting to tell the police before they paid over the ransom money, but he also confided that the twins weren't returned after the money was paid.'

'We're pretty sure that the kidnapping was a ruse, in order to extort money from the wife's private family trust,' Jack added.

'Was the wife in on it, and does that explain her silence on the subject?' Esther asked.

Percy nodded. 'That's one of the things I need you to find out. During your professional visits to the house, pick up anything you can that suggests, one way or the other, whether the mother was in on the kidnapping of her own twin sons.'

'And that's all?' Esther said suspiciously.

'If you learn anything more about Emily's disappearance, that'll be a bonus,' Percy added, 'particularly for your friend Alice.'

'And I pass anything I get on to Jack? Or is this a devious scheme to get more roast lamb suppers?'

'Thought you'd never get around to making this a weekly arrangement,' Percy replied, smiling. 'What's for pudding?'

Chapter Thirteen

'How are our guests enjoying our fine cuisine?' Percy enquired with heavy sarcasm as he walked past the front desk, then stopped on a hand signal from the sergeant.

'The girl seems very grateful fer the best cell in the place an' the chop 'ouse down the road's enjoyin' the increased custom, but Inspector Mitchell wants ter know who's payin'. An' as fer Martha Crabbe, we'd all deem it a great favour if yer'd get 'er moved ter the jail. She's been charged like yer instructed, so she shouldn't be 'ere any longer an' she's givin' us all grief. Apart from the shoutin' an' carryin'-on, she spits like an alleycat.'

'Women show their affections in different ways,' Percy replied, chuckling, 'but you've just given me an idea. Is she in one of those cells with bars instead of a door?'

'Yeah, mainly so we can see what she's up ter when we goes down there wi' 'er food.'

'Has she been fed this morning?'

'No, not yet.'

'Very good. I'll be back down in a few minutes for her bread and lard.'

'Bugger off!' was Martha's initial response when Percy appeared in front of her bars.

'Nice to see you again too, Martha. I take it you don't want this fine repast?'

'Shove it up yer arse!'

'Tut tut! And here I was, all prepared to discuss a little arrangement under which I'd drop the current charge against you — which, remember, would qualify you for an appointment with the public hangman — and have you transferred to Newgate, where the food's better.'

'What yer got in mind?'

'Well, this may sound a little unusual, coming from someone in my profession, but I want you to agree to be transferred out of here into Newgate and then send word to Mangler Maguire that you want to be rescued.'

'An' why would I do that?'

'I just told you. A reduced charge — perhaps no charge at all, depending on the outcome — and a change of scenery. But if Mr Maguire *does* accept your request for a rescue, don't expect to be out for long.'

'Yer plannin' summat, aren't yer?'

'Obviously, but that's for me to know and you to wonder. But from your perspective, it's the only show in town at the moment. Do we have a deal?'

'Yeah, but if Mangler decides ter do me in once 'e gets me out…'

'Yes, I know,' Percy joked, 'you'll never speak to me again.'

'Do you have any references?' Millicent Mallory enquired over the lip of her tea cup at Esther seated across the low table from her.

'I haven't worked for some time, as I explained,' Esther replied in what she hoped was the right mixture of eagerness and deference. 'Before I was married, I was employed in a garment factory in Spitalfields, but unfortunately the proprietor died shortly after I left. I've had several replies to my letters, but there's no-one as yet who could confirm my ability.'

Millicent reached across to the settee at her side and handed Esther a child's nursery bib that contained an inch-long tear. Then she put down her tea cup, stood up and walked to a small wicker basket on a low table by the window from which she extracted a needle with a length of thread already attached. She handed it to Esther with a smile.

'I won't need any references, if you can show me how good you are with this.'

Esther lost no time in running a perfect line of holding stiches down the tear as she smiled down at the garment.

'You have small children?'

'Just two into their double figures now. Lawrence is thirteen and Lydia's just turned eleven. If I employ you, one of your tasks would be to teach her how to sew and darn. At present her world seems to revolve around those dreadful novel things that are really not appropriate for a young lady of breeding.'

'Some would say that neither is being a seamstress,' Esther smiled deprecatingly. 'Have you something more challenging than this child's bib?'

'I have a tea blouse with fraying around the cuff,' Millicent replied. 'May I go and get it for you?'

'Yes, please do.' Esther smiled eagerly, then took a good look round the sitting room while her prospective employer was out. On a side cabinet was a photograph of two grinning infants, beaming out at the world from some sort of pushchair. It hadn't gone yellow yet, like the few that Esther had seen in the past had done, so she could assume that it had been taken fairly recently. There was a bustle in the doorway and Millicent Mallory reappeared carrying an elegant silk blouse.

'I'm quite fond of this,' she advised Esther, 'but as you can see, it's become badly worn with use.'

'Would I be permitted to cut it?' Esther asked.

Millicent nodded. 'Provided that you know what you're doing.'

With a reassuring smile, Esther asked for the workbasket on the nearby table, then set about cutting the cuff from its join with the lower sleeve and reversing the material before re-sewing it using a thread of approximately the same colour as the blouse. Millicent's eyebrows rose in admiration and she smiled broadly as she advised Esther that her services had just been acquired.

'Thank you very much,' Esther replied humbly.

'We haven't discussed the details, of course,' Millicent reminded her, 'but I'd initially require you here once a week. The girl who used to do this sort of work walked out on us without warning some weeks ago now and there's quite a bit to catch up on. If it's convenient for you, I'd like you to come on Wednesdays, since I have a weekly bridge club on that day and our meetings sometimes run late. It would be convenient to have you here when the children get home from school and of course you could then begin teaching Lydia what she needs to learn. I'll pay whatever your professional rates are, per garment, and you could start this coming Wednesday, if that would be convenient?'

'Definitely!' Esther enthused as she stood up to leave. 'Next Wednesday, then.'

On the appointed day, Esther presented herself, carrying her own sewing box and was immediately set to work with a pile of assorted pieces of running repair, from a boy's school jacket to a ball gown that needed to be let out at the bust. She'd been at it for two hours or so, seated at the sitting room table, when a maid delivered tea and biscuits and was followed into the room by Millicent Mallory, who invited Esther to take a break and share tea with her.

'Tell me about your own children,' Millicent invited her and Esther was grateful that she was not required to invent a family for the occasion.

'My eldest is a girl called Lillian, but we just call her Lily. She's four now, and I have a two-year-old called Bertie.'

'Is that short for Albert? It's become such a popular name since the Queen married her handsome prince.'

'Yes, I think that's why we chose it,' Esther confirmed. 'My husband and I are such admirers of the Queen and her beautiful family.'

'What does your husband do for a living?'

'He's employed in an insurance brokerage,' Esther lied. 'He's only a junior clerk at present, but he hopes to climb the ladder over the years and perhaps finish up as a broker himself.'

'Hence the need for you to supplement the family income with your own skills.' Millicent nodded with a degree of condescension. 'I'm very fortunate that my own husband is a highly successful lawyer in The Strand. Lord Combermere is one of his clients.'

'You must have been very young when you had your children, if I might make so bold,' Esther said in the hope of drawing the conversation in the desired direction. 'You don't appear to be much older than thirty, although I'm sure you must be.'

'I'm thirty-six,' Millicent advised her, clearly flattered. 'It helps to have your children when you're younger, I believe. I have friends of my own age who have ballooned out quite alarmingly through having their third or fourth when in their thirties. Now, if I might revert to more mundane matters, could you get Lydia to take off her school dress when she comes in and hand it to you? The hem's hanging after one of her boisterous games at her school and it makes her look such a drudge. If they continue to tolerate that sort of thing, we'll be obliged to change her school. Now, since you seem to have enough to occupy you for the time being, I'll go up and change ahead of my weekly appointment at my bridge club. They serve a light luncheon there, so I'll be eating out, but I'll ask cook to send you in some sandwiches later on.'

'Thank you very much,' Esther replied dutifully, then changed her seat for the comfortable one near the front window, from which she could watch comings and goings.

An hour later, while munching appreciatively on a salmon sandwich, she saw a man she took to be the family coachman walk from round the side of the building to what appeared to be the stables and lead out a horse which he attached to a brougham. A few minutes later Millicent Mallory stepped out from the front door and the coachman opened the coach's side door with a slight bow of respect as Millicent climbed in, immaculately dressed in a blue outdoor coat with matching feathered hat and gloves. The coachman slapped the reins and the carriage ground down the gravel drive into the side road beyond, turning left towards the main road.

Less than thirty minutes later, Esther looked up in surprise as she heard the coach returning and watched the coachman reverse his earlier actions before disappearing back down the side of the house, where he presumably had his accommodation. Shortly after that the maid appeared to retrieve the leftovers from Esther's snack and smiled as she saw the flowered shawl that Esther was working on.

'I wish *I* could sew like that. Me Ma always promised ter teach me, but then she ran off when I were only twelve, leavin' just me and me Da. I'm Jane, by the way.'

'Esther. I'm only here for the day, doing some sewing work for the family.'

'Would you like some more tea?'

'Thank you, that would be nice. How long have you worked here?'

'About a year now. They're good ter me an' the family's lovely. I never 'ad no bruvvers an' sisters, yer see.'

'I bet you'd have liked a couple of baby brothers like those charming angels in that photograph,' Esther ventured.

Jane's face fell. 'They was lovely, them two — always smilin' an' chucklin'. I 'ope they find 'em afore much longer.'

'Are they missing?' Esther asked casually.

Jane's face turned a bright red. 'Forget what I said, please, only we're not s'posed ter mention 'em, 'cos the Master gets upset.'

'And the Mistress?'

'Not 'er, as far as I've noticed. It's like she don't miss 'em. But yer won't say that I mentioned owt?'

'Of course not and thank you again for the sandwiches.'

'Thank the cook fer them. I'll get yer that tea.'

Shortly before five in the afternoon, Esther met the older children of the family as they tumbled into the sitting room, panting and sweating from having run all the way up the road, arguing volubly about who had won the race. The boy was the first to spot Esther in the seat by the window and he smiled condescendingly in the manner no doubt taught to him by his parents.

'Oh, hello there. You must be the new sewing girl. Do you do shirts?'

'I do anything, provided that they're washed first. You must be Lawrence.'

'That's me, Father's son and heir. And this scarecrow who can't run as fast as me is Lydia.'

'Hello, Lydia,' Esther said in her most conspiratorial voice. 'Your mother advises me that you have a school dress with a hem that needs to be taken up.'

'That's right,' Lydia smiled precociously, 'but I'm not taking it off here, so that Lawrence can see my petticoats.'

'Who'd want to see *your* petticoats?' Lawrence sneered, 'and in any case I'm going out to play cricket against the garden wall. I'll let whatshername fix your dress.'

'My name's Esther,' the 'sewing girl' advised Lydia. 'Come closer and I'll see if I can tack that fallen hem up while you stand there, without any need for you to take the dress off.' As she began working on the hem, Esther made a casual enquiry. 'Who used to do your sewing before I was engaged?'

'That was Emily, our governess and nanny.'

'You're surely too old to need a nanny?'

'Yes of course, she was really here to look after — well anyway, she did our sewing.'

'There seems to be an awful lot to catch up on. How did this hem get pulled down?'

'That was my friend Lettie. We were racing each other up a wall and she tried to grab me and almost missed. The dress came off second best when her hand slipped.'

'Hardly seemly behaviour for a young lady who'll one day take her place in society.'

'I know, but I seem to always want to play rough games. Have you finished?'

'Yes. Do you have anything else that needs to be repaired?'

'Probably, but that'll have to wait. I want to read some more of my novel before supper. Thank you, by the way. Will you be here next week?'

'I hope so,' Esther replied, well satisfied with her first day's work.

By the end of the third week, as they sat around the lamb roast that Jack was carving and that seemed to have become a standard feature of their Fridays, Esther was querying whether or not she was still required to spy on the Mallory family.

'Surely, I've got all you need. Millicent Mallory's in denial that she ever had twin boys, the servants have been sworn to silence, as have their rather over-indulged older children, and the lady of the house attends a bridge club every Wednesday, which can't be far away, given that the coachman's always back from delivering her within half an hour.'

'So, fifteen minutes there and fifteen minutes back,' Percy mused out loud. 'But how do we know that she's going to a bridge club?'

'We don't, clearly,' Esther conceded, 'but what are you suggesting? That she's got a secret lover or something?'

'We don't know that she doesn't,' Percy reminded her. 'And there's a railway station not fifteen minutes away by coach. From there she could travel to anywhere in London. I'm just wondering if she's got the twins hidden away somewhere and is visiting them every week.'

'Well, I can hardly follow her while I'm supposed to be doing her sewing, can I?'

'No,' Percy said, deep in thought. Then his eyes switched to Jack. 'Feel like testing the limitations of your leg?'

'Sergeant Ballantyne's convinced I'm a lead-swinger and if I start taking afternoons off he'll have me out of the force in no time.'

'You'd only need to follow her once,' Percy argued.

Jack shook his head vigorously. 'Not even once! I'm not going to become your hired sniffer dog. I'm supposed to be on light duties, resting a healing broken leg.'

'And bored to screaming point?' Percy persevered.

'Of *course* bored to screaming point, but until they decide that I'm fit enough to resume normal duties, that's where I'm stuck. And whatever became of my promotion, eh?'

'I can think of no better way of proving your fitness and your suitability for promotion, than assisting in the location and rescue of two kidnapped children,' Percy persisted.

'Who're helpless little mites even younger than your own son,' Esther added.

Jack glared round the kitchen in search of a suitable response, or — miraculously — a voice in his support. Uncle Percy was bad enough, but when Esther joined in on his side it was like trying to open a parasol in a force nine gale. He shrugged with resignation, then tried one last card as he glared at Percy.

'Why can't you do it?'

'I'm off to see a man about a jail break,' Percy replied with a slow smile.

'I still don't see how I can be expected to follow the woman with a broken leg,' Jack complained.

'She doesn't have a broken leg,' Esther joked, then stopped smiling when she realised that Jack had a point. Millicent Mallory travelled in a coach, whereas Jack would be on foot — and literally, in his case. One foot only.

'Even if I could keep up with the coach,' Jack added, 'I'd be pretty obvious, haring down the road like a one-legged racehorse.'

'Then maybe you should take a coach of your own and follow hers,' Esther suggested half-heartedly, although even she could see the flaws in that arrangement.

'So, I sit outside her own house, in a coach of my own, then when hers comes out I instruct my coachman to "follow that coach", only to pull up behind it and pay off my coachman wherever we finish up? How do I know she doesn't always transfer to another coach or something, or take the train?'

'Suppose you were to hitch a ride on *her* coach?' Esther suggested.

Jack snorted in derision. 'Do you not think the coachman might spot me, sitting on the baggage rail on the roof? Or should I stand at the side of the road with a loaded pistol, flag down the coach and demand a ride in it?'

'How about hanging on to the back?'

'Only naughty children do that sort of thing and sometimes they fall off and get injured. And *they* have the use of two legs.'

'Can you think of a better plan?'

'Yes — that we abandon the whole idea.'

Esther gave him a look.

'How do I know that the coach has something on the back for me to hold onto?' Jack said with a sigh.

'Leave that to me,' Esther replied. 'And if it does, it's your turn to play the daredevil. That way, you won't be shown up by your own wife.'

The following day, Esther turned up for duty at the Mallory household and smiled with forced gratitude while Millicent counted out into her hand the coins due to her for the garments she'd done work on the previous week, 'plus a little extra for your trouble in showing Lydia how to stitch up a hem'. Then it was another round of working on a pile of repairs and alterations, smiling and gritting her teeth through Millicent's condescending drivel, all about herself, her husband's status in his profession, the older children's superiority at their private schools, and her own preference for carrot juice for maintaining a youthful complexion. Then the tricky part, once morning tea and biscuits had been consumed and Millicent was about to retire upstairs to beautify herself.

'Since it's such a lovely day outside,' Esther asked in a suitably humble voice, 'would you mind if I took a chair out to that lovely little summer house on the lawn and did my sewing out there?'

'Of course not, my dear, but don't sit out there for too long, exposed to the heat like that. You have such delicate skin and it would be shame to coarsen it.'

As Millicent descended the front steps, Esther was already established in the summer house, with a clear view of the coach as it was driven slowly into place. By craning her neck she was able to see round the back of it and she smiled.

Chapter Fourteen

'The men are gettin' restless,' Percy was advised and he could hardly blame them in the circumstances. This was their fifth night out in the early autumn chill, concealed in doorways, side alleys and wagons, or hiding around corners, all with a view of the main gate of Newgate Prison. The men had been instructed not to move and were not even allowed to smoke, in case the light from their pipes, cigars or cigarettes gave away their positions.

'Tell them "tough luck" and at least they get the days off,' Percy muttered, as he grimly anticipated yet another screaming match with Inspector Mitchell the following day, regarding the absence of men on the streets following nights in which their duty hours were wasted watching the jail entrance for signs of an escape bid. Then there were the 'overtime' payments to add to the cost of keeping Clara Manders fed, in her 'special' cell, with a daily intake of shop-bought meals that were probably of a far higher quality than she could expect to enjoy if she were granted her freedom.

But hopefully it was all going to be worth it, if only to expose the corruption inside Newgate and the ease with which the regime could be subverted, either if the money was right or those employed inside there had dark secrets that they could not afford to have revealed by those who knew them and could exploit them to their own advantage. They might even be able to buckle some of Maguire's leading lieutenants and put a temporary stop to some of his more nefarious activities. Then at least Percy would have something to show for the worrying expense he was incurring simply on a 'gut feeling'.

Suddenly there was movement at the front gate and the clear moonlight at long last revealed what they had been waiting for all week, as a wagon could be heard rumbling around the corner of Old Bailey. The gate creaked open a little wider and the face of a turnkey could be seen squinting out into the street, almost skeletal in the moonlight as he sought to ensure that all was clear. The wagon came to a halt and a tall man wrapped in a heavy cloak stepped down from the front board and approached the now half open gate, where a short stout figure could be seen just behind the turnkey.

Percy shook the rattle hard in the pre-arranged signal and police officers in ordinary workmen's clothes ran in from all directions towards the gate. A hasty attempt to close it was blocked by three officers who held it open while two more seized hold of the two figures just inside it, each man to their pre-designated target. The big man in the cloak had knocked three men down until someone had the presence of mind to whack him on the back of the head with a billy club and he went down like a bag of coal. Percy gave instructions for the other man with him to be buckled, then looked down with a gleeful grin at the unconscious form of Michael Maguire.

'Buckle him at the wrists *and* the ankles, then throw him into the paddy wagon when it gets here and two of you sit on him all the way back to the shop. One on his chest and the other on his legs. If he comes round and struggles, send him into dreamland again.'

'Can we kill 'im?' one of his men asked.

'Definitely not,' Percy replied with a vicious leer, 'I have other plans for him, although the net result will be the same, one way or another.'

He walked over to where two more of his men had the turnkey and Martha Crabbe firmly held, but still conscious, since neither of them had offered any resistance. He smiled at Martha Crabbe and she spat on the ground at his feet.

'Always the lady.' He grinned as he stepped backwards. He looked at the constable who was holding her firmly by the arm. 'Does she smell as bad as I imagine?'

''Fraid so, Sergeant.'

'Well, you'd better let go of her, before you catch something.'

'But she'll get away then,' the constable objected.

'Do you fancy holding on to her all the way back in an already crowded paddy wagon?'

'Definitely not, Sergeant.'

'Then let her go and let's pretend that she kneed you in the groin.'

'She did, one time, when we was loadin' her inter the 'oldin' cell.'

'You must be Constable Preece, that right?' Percy grinned.

'Yes, Sergeant.'

'Well smack her around the head, *then* let her go.'

The constable did as instructed and as Martha picked herself off the ground she made a run for it down Old Bailey.

Percy grinned as he watched her skid round the far corner and into the cover of darkness, then turned his attention to the paddy wagon that had finally appeared, summoned from where it had been hidden behind a warehouse gate a few streets away.

'Throw 'em in on top of each other,' he instructed, 'while I go and get the turnkey.'

'Am I bein' taken in?' the turnkey asked.

Percy nodded. 'Eventually, but first I think we'll get the Deputy Keeper out of his bed.'

Back at the station, at the ungodly hour of three am, Percy made himself a mug of tea and took it back to his office, where he sat waiting, blowing pipe smoke contentedly up towards the ceiling. His patience and foresight were rewarded when a uniformed constable tapped politely on his open door.

'One o' the blokes yer brought in earlier wants ter talk ter yer. 'E's down in Number Three.'

'Thank you, Constable,' Percy replied as he rose from behind his desk with a satisfied grin and tapped out the residue from his pipe bowl into the ashtray in front of him. Two minutes later he was looking intently through a set of bars at the anxious face of an overweight scruff with a large lump forming on his left temple.

Percy smiled. 'I don't believe I've had the pleasure, Mr ...?'

'Venables. 'Arry Venables. I bin charged wi' five murders, as well as ternight's little caper. That can't be right, can it? Yer gets dropped fer Murder an' I ain't done none.'

'That must have been my mistake, Mr Venables. But it was an easy one to make, in the circumstances. You were arrested in the company of a Mr Maguire, also known as "Truegood" and quite rightly also known as "Mangler". Since I strongly suspect him of those five murders in question — and I think we both know which ones I'm talking about — I can only assume that those persons discovered in his company were also involved.'

'They was all down ter Mangler — honest! 'E always liked ter do 'em 'imself, wi' a sledge'ammer an' all we did was search out the victims an' make sure they was surrounded when 'e did 'em.'

'I'm no lawyer, Mr Venables, but in my book that makes you an accomplice to the murders and the hangman makes no allowances when calculating the drop.'

'Can I not "turn Queen's evidence" or wha'ever it's called?'

Percy studied his terrified face for a moment as he appeared to think the proposal over carefully.

'You puzzle me, Mr Venables. In the entire six weeks or so that I've been soiling my boot leather in this particular part of our world-famous city I've not come across a single soul who was prepared to peach on Mangler Maguire, given his reputation. What makes you so different?'

'It's better than 'angin' like a dog. An' if Maguire takes the drop, there'll be no more danger from 'im. 'Alf the blokes what runs wi' 'im — meself included — wanted out weeks ago, but we daresen't in case we was next.'

'Did you know that Mr Maguire was due to be launched into eternity last year, but managed to bribe his way out of Newgate?'

'So 'e told us, but we wasn't sure an' we wasn't prepared ter risk peachin' on 'im, in case we was wrong.'

'You mentioned five murders earlier,' Percy reminded him. 'It just so happens that I'm investigating precisely that number. Were you present at all of them?'

'Yeah, but like I said, it were Mangler what done 'em. We was only there ter prevent any escape.'

'And you'd be prepared to testify to that in a court of law?'

'If I do, will they 'ang me?'

'Not if you stick to your story and a smart lawyer of my acquaintance — name of Charlie Gill — tells the court that you only did what you did out of fear of Maguire. I believe that lawyers call it "duress" and you might walk away altogether. At worst, probably only three or four years.'

'It's a deal!' Venables agreed as the colour began to return to his face. 'When does I get ter go ter court?'

'First things first,' Percy advised him. 'I'm going to have you escorted back upstairs, you're going to tell me all about the murders you witnessed, while I write it all down, then you're going to sign what I've written. Can you sign your own name?'

'Sorta,' Venables advised him, 'but I can't read nowt.'

'That won't be necessary,' Percy grinned, 'since I'll take great pleasure in reading it all back to you.'

'And then I'll be kept separate from Mangler? I wouldn't want 'im ter get at me, either 'ere or in Newgate. An' 'e's got a lot o' friends in Newgate.'

'Don't worry, Mr Venables,' Percy reassured him. 'Once you've signed on the dotted, I'll be very surprised if Mr Maguire makes it as far as Newgate.'

Chapter Fifteen

The next day being Wednesday, Esther was back to playing the seamstress, but this time with her heart even more firmly in her mouth than it had been on the previous occasions. She sat resignedly through more of Millicent Mallory's patronising conversation and imperious instructions during morning tea and biscuits, then as soon as she excused herself in order to go upstairs and change ahead of her bridge club appointment, Esther transferred to the window seat and gazed anxiously out into the garden.

As arranged, she waved her white handkerchief in a signal and was very relieved to see a hand wave back to her reassuringly from the shrubbery, where Jack was hopefully well concealed. She held her breath as she saw him scuttle, head down, through the tangle of rhododendrons towards the stable block in which the brougham was kept, hoping that no-one else was gazing out of a front window, upstairs or down. The children were at school as usual and hopefully Jane and the cook would be busy in the kitchen, leaving only the coachman, Stanniforth, who was probably donning his riding coat in his own quarters, while Millicent Mallory was upstairs, preparing to look her elegant best.

Jack reached the safety of the stables, prayed softly, then let out his breath in relief when he found the door unlocked. The horse whinnied slightly and shuffled in its stall as he slipped down in front of it to where the carriage was stored, then walked round to the back of it, hoping upon hope that Esther had correctly described it to him based on her fleeting observation of it.

She'd been right, as always, and there was a sort of wooden bar above the rear wheel axle and two rods projecting from the rear of the passenger section that would do nicely for hand-holds. He hooked his walking stick over one arm and climbed onto the wooden bar; then he gripped both hand-holds firmly as he waited. After a few moments he heard the sounds of the horse being attached to the front end and held his breath as he prayed that he would not give away his hiding place by coughing and that Stanniforth would not choose this day of all days to inspect the rear of the coach.

Millicent Mallory did her usual stately walk down the front steps to the coach and Stanniforth held the door open for her with his usual bow. From inside the sitting room Esther gritted her teeth and tried not to scream with frustration as each second ticked by during which Jack would be exposed, hanging on to the rear of the coach as it sat on the semi-circular front drive. Esther couldn't see him because the coach was not yet in line with the sitting room window, but anyone looking out of a front window further down the driveway would be perfectly positioned to see that the vehicle had a stowaway and sound the alarm.

She let out a long-held breath as the coach moved off and she saw Jack clinging for dear life to the back of it. Fortunately, there were no other coaches on Heath Street and Stanniforth swung his to the left as usual, minimising the short period of time during which Jack was clearly visible from all parts of the house. As the coach disappeared behind the line of yew hedge, Esther whispered a brief prayer of gratitude and went back to her sewing.

Jack was praying for totally different reasons as he clung precariously to the rear of the brougham, feeling every rut and jolt through his still healing leg as they trundled down the side street towards the main road, where he would of course become visible to anyone who cared to look. He was banking on the fact that it was not unheard of for young children to hitch rides on the backs of coaches in this manner, although he'd never heard of sober adults trying the same trick and it was barely midday according to the massive clock tower that they passed as they rumbled down Hampstead Road towards the city.

Suddenly the coach came to a halt outside the railway station and Jack just had time to leap clear of the coach, his injured leg screaming in painful protest as he landed on it at the wrong angle, while Stanniforth climbed down and made a big fuss of opening the door for Millicent to descend into the roadway with a loud instruction that the coachman was to return to collect her at around seven that evening.

Jack hobbled as fast as he could behind her as she approached the station ticket window and demanded a return ticket to Kentish Town. Jack ordered a single ticket to the same destination, only two places in the queue behind her, then followed her like a shadow along the somewhat rickety footbridge and down onto the platform. Inevitably, Millicent was travelling First Class, but Jack knew where to alight and two stops later he jumped off as he heard the porter announce in a loud voice that they had reached Kentish Town.

Once outside, Millicent led him on a determined stride through a tangle of local streets that slowly become more salubrious the further they walked from the station, until they eventually turned into Burghley Road. Jack's leg was on the point of giving up on him completely and he was in the process of cursing Uncle Percy for the fiftieth time when Millicent turned sharply into the entrance to a splendidly appointed three storey terraced house that stood back from the street behind a set of wrought iron railings.

Jack crossed the road and leaned for support against a gas lamp pole in order to obtain a better look, just as the front door was drawn back and a liveried footman of some sort bowed in respect as Millicent swept into the front entrance, handing her hat to the flunky as she progressed down the thickly carpeted hall. Jack just had time to witness a tall gentleman enter the hall from a side room and embrace Millicent before the front door was shut and his mission was accomplished.

Slowly Jack crossed the road and made a note of the house number, then leaned heavily on the front railings, regaining his breath and standing on one leg to relieve the pressure on the broken one. He was looking up and down as he did so and from the corner of his eye he caught movement in a room one floor up. Millicent and the same man who had welcomed her into the house appeared to be warmly embracing behind what they no doubt believed was the anonymity of a lace curtain, but someone had left the window open and the curtain was blowing slightly in the early afternoon breeze.

Thoroughly relieved and contented with his afternoon's work, Jack made his way back to Whitehall by bus, bracing himself for more biting verbal abuse from Sergeant Ballantyne for his excessively long dinner break from the tedium of his work in Records.

Percy was dog tired after yet another sleepless night, but he had urgent work to do and for once he was going to thoroughly enjoy it. In one pub after another he spread the joyful tidings that Mangler Maguire had at long last been buckled and that sometime that afternoon he might be viewed and cheered on as he was led down the front steps of Bethnal Green Police Station to a waiting Black Maria and a custodial existence in Newgate until he faced trial on five counts of Murder. This was simply to square the books, Percy assured them, since even if the jury by some miracle acquitted him of those charges, he still awaited a somewhat adjourned appointment with James Berry, the troubadour of the trapdoor, in respect of his previous conviction, much delayed in its aftermath.

A sizeable crowd had already gathered in the road outside as Percy ordered the coachman at the reins of the Black Maria to draw it up on the far side from the station entrance, 'so that the relatives of those he murdered can get a better view.'

'That's against regulations,' the driver reminded him. 'What's yer authority fer that?'

'Five murder victims,' Percy advised him as he walked back inside to order the escort party out into the street.

They still had Maguire securely buckled at both his wrists and his ankles and he made a faintly ludicrous spectacle as he half shuffled, half hobbled, towards the paddy wagon, his once impressive height no longer an advantage as he was forced to double over in order to make progress across the rutted roadway, through two jeering lines of those whose fear had now become black hatred.

Suddenly there was a shout from a burly man on the front row who was concealing something by his side.

'Yer killed innocent folk an' left the poor bastards in the rubble. But the rubble's gonna take its revenge now!'

He raised his arm to reveal a sizeable piece of broken masonry and hurled it at Maguire's head, which it struck with a sickening thud. Maguire stumbled, but remained upright, as blood poured from a gash on his forehead, but the first missile had been the signal for a flurry of lumps of brick, tile, concrete and metal piping that struck Maguire on every conceivable part of his body like a hail of arrows in a Medieval archery storm. Maguire sank to his knees as a hand came through the front row of the incensed mob. The hand contained a sledgehammer, which the burly woman swung at his bowed head, smashing it like a soft boiled egg.

A howl of appreciation rose up, as if an unpopular gladiator had just died in the Coliseum and the woman raced up the street surrounded by a large crowd obviously intent on giving her cover as she made good her escape. The constables who had been leading Maguire to the wagon and who had fled at the throwing of the first lump of brick, now raced back down the front steps of the police station and retrieved Maguire's inert form from the roadway, dragging it back indoors to loud oaths and yells of triumph from the mob. Percy leaned against the Black Maria, lit his pipe and smiled.

'You planned that, didn't you?' Inspector Mitchell yelled, red faced, as he burst into Percy's office twenty minutes later.

Percy looked up unconcerned. 'How can you plan a spontaneous street riot?'

'You know what I mean. You deliberately ordered that paddy wagon to the other side of the road, knowing what the mob would do to our prisoner!'

'Yes and no,' Percy replied calmly. 'I ordered the wagon to the other side of the road, certainly, but only in order that those who've lived in fear of Maguire for the past few months could be assured that we had him securely in custody.'

'A likely story! You know he's dead, I suppose?'

'That happy intelligence was brought to me a few minutes ago.' Percy smiled seraphically.

'And now we've got no-one to put on trial for five murders, you imbecile! I was warned about you before you even arrived here. Every person who you're convinced is guilty of a capital crime finishes up dead before they get to court, as if you regard yourself as some sort of avenging angel. How are we supposed to close the books on these five murders?'

'Read the statement obligingly dictated to me by Mr Venables. He was there on each occasion and since Maguire is no longer available for trial for the main offences, we'd be well advised not to try putting Venables on trial as his accomplice.'

'So, what do we charge him with?'

'His part in the prison break. But let me speak to him first, because he holds vital information regarding another matter that I'm investigating.'

Back down in the cell area, Venables was just as eager to talk as he had been on the previous occasion.

'Is it true what they're sayin' — that Mangler's dead? Why am I still down 'ere an' not in Newgate?'

'First things first, Mr Venables. It's correct that your former partner in crime Mr Maguire was unfortunately stoned to death by the mob in a somewhat Biblical fashion. Which means, of course, that we only have you left to answer for those murders that you conveniently signed up for.'

'Yer bastard! Yer promised me that Mangler'd be the one ter cop fer them an' that I'd get off light!'

'That might still be possible, Mr Venables,' Percy assured him with a sick grin. 'But only "might". In fact, I might consider doing you just for your part in the jailbreak and forgetting all about the murders, in exchange for some information which for me is very important, but to you might seem trivial.'

'Like what? Tell me whatever yer wanna know an' I'll tell yer, if it means I only get done for the breakout.'

'The final murder — at least I hope it was the final one,' Percy began. 'The girl in Short Street. Were you a witness to that one?'

'O' course, like I told yer the other day. What about it?'

'Who was she, exactly?'

'A daft lass called Clara Manders.'

'You sure about that?'

'Sure I'm sure — I knew her, didn' I?'

'Go on, then — tell me all about her.'

'She lived up Shoreditch way an' she weren't right in the 'ead, if yer know what I mean. She shoulda bin a nun or somefin', 'cos she was always goin' on about God and the Virgin Mary. But she were barmy — yer know? One time she reckoned she talked ter an angel what were sittin' on the church spire.'

'So why did Mangler want her dead?'

'Ah well, yer see, she got it in 'er 'ead that God were wantin' ter punish Mangler fer all 'is sins an' she took ter preachin' on a box outside the local theatre, callin' on folks ter rise up against 'im in the name o' the Lord. She couldn't see what sorta danger she were creatin' for 'erself.'

'So Mangler silenced her?'

'Yeah. One night me an' another bloke broke inter the doss 'ouse where she were livin' an' took 'er out inter the yard, where Mangler done 'er in wi' this big 'ammer what 'e always used. Then we put 'er in a wheelbarrer an' took 'er down ter Short Street an' dumped 'er in the rubble. But we was told to make out it were a girl called Emily Broome what we'd done fer. That were another lass what Mangler knew an' she give 'im 'er 'andbag ter leave near the body.'

'So you're quite sure it was Clara Manders who was killed?'

'Dead sure — like I said, I knew 'er. Pretty enough lass, but definitely a slate loose.'

'So, the body in the rubble definitely wasn't Emily Broome?'

'It were made ter look like 'er, but Mangler said 'e needed 'er fer summat else.'

'Thank you very much, Mr Venables. You can expect to be transferred to Newgate later this morning, charged only with your part in the attempt to spring Martha Crabbe.'

Venables beamed back at him and seemed to sag with relief. 'Yer a real gent, Mr Enright, an' I'll make sure ter tell all me friends that.'

Chapter Sixteen

'Great news about Maguire,' Jack confirmed as he poured the wine that Percy had just uncorked, 'and thanks again for the wine. The roast should be out of the oven in a few minutes. That right, Esther?'

'Only if Uncle Percy confirms that my days as a seamstress to that dreadful Millicent Mallory are over,' Esther sniffed as she laid out the cutlery and reached for her own glass of wine, raising it in the air. 'Here's to the fact that I no longer need to earn my living with a needle and thread. From now on it'll be just Jack's rips and cuts, although while he's been doing a desk job they've been kept to a minimum. That said, he must have got some grease from the back of the coach on his trouser turn-ups and I'm not sure how to get that out.'

'You did well there, Jack,' Percy assured him, 'and it may come as no surprise to you when you learn whose address it was that you followed Millicent Mallory to.'

'I'll take a guess at Victor Bradley,' Jack suggested.

Percy nodded. 'You wouldn't need the talents of a Nostradamus to work that out, but you're right.'

Jack picked up the carving set that had been a wedding present and clattered the knife against the long fork in a silent gesture for Esther to remove the lamb roast from the oven.

'What did your last slave die of?' she said sarcastically.

'Something she caught off the grease from my trouser turn-ups,' Jack quipped back. 'Uncle Percy, would I be able to claim the cleaning bill from the Met?'

'Certainly, if you could explain why you were lurking outside a house in Kentish Town when you were supposed to be head down in Records.'

The next few minutes were taken up in the removal of the roast from the oven, the carving of it into slices, the placing of the vegetables in the centre of the table and several expressions of appreciation of Esther's cooking skills from mouths full of lamb, potatoes, carrots and gravy. Esther was the first to clear her mouth sufficiently for speech, mainly because she had eaten less.

'You still haven't confirmed my release from sewing duties for that awful Millicent Mallory, Uncle Percy.'

Percy cleared his mouth and smiled. 'Most certainly, but you still haven't quite completed your service to the Metropolitan Police.'

'My *unpaid* service, you mean?'

'How would you like a companion, baby sitter, domestic assistant and friend?' he asked.

'Isn't that why I married Jack? And what makes you think that the next experiment will be any more successful than the last? But are you serious?'

'I think so.'

'We don't have any room for a live-in domestic.'

'You won't need one, trust me. Only there's a girl currently being accommodated in Bethnal Green Police Station in need of a kindly soul to take her under their wing and lead her from the darkness of her current life into a bright shining future among real people who actually care about her.'

'You should have been a poet,' Jack remarked admiringly.

'You should also stop speaking nonsense.' Esther pouted. 'What are you up to *this* time?'

'Just trust me and take this girl in hand when I release her,' Percy requested. 'I want you to accompany her to what passes for her home, find her somewhere to wash and smarten herself up, then see if you can't find suitable clothes for her and bring her back here.'

'I already told you that we don't have the accommodation. How much is this all going to cost?'

Percy reached for his wallet and extracted a banknote. 'Here's ten pounds. Let me know if you spend more.'

'You're serious, aren't you?' Esther said.

Percy nodded. 'You'll have to trust me. Have I ever misled you?'

'Which of those several occasions do you wish to discuss first?'

Jack decided to intervene. 'I feel sure you haven't finished with me.'

'No indeed I haven't,' Percy confirmed. 'I hope I'm not the only one who's inclined to the theory that when Mrs Mallory goes to that house in Kentish Town, it's not just to meet her lover Mr Bradley. She's got her twins hidden away in there, almost certainly. That's why she hasn't displayed any obvious distress regarding their official disappearance. They haven't disappeared at all.'

'So, we keep watch on the place?' Jack asked.

Percy shook his head. 'They wouldn't be that stupid. The children are still tiny and can be tucked away somewhere in a back room, well out of sight. They're hardly likely to take them down the street in a perambulator, are they?'

'Then what do you suggest?'

'You mentioned that when you looked up, you saw the two of them in an upstairs room, embracing?'

'Yes, but that just suggests that they're lovers. What's that got to do with our gaining access to the house in order to locate the twins?'

'Well, supposing that when you were looking up at the window, quite casually, you'd seen the man attempting to strangle the woman? What would you, as a law-abiding citizen, have done?'

'Called the police, obviously and they ... oh, *now* I get it.'

'Next Wednesday, at around three in the afternoon.' Percy grinned at Jack, as Esther shook her head in exasperation.

Chapter Seventeen

Jack stood uncertainly outside number 37 Burghley Road, then gave a sigh of relief as several police wagons rumbled around the corner and came to a halt. Uniformed officers piled out of the backs of them, four of them carrying a heavy iron bar that had four handles attached in order that the bar could be used in a forward motion to smash down doors. Percy alighted from the passenger side of the lead vehicle and raised his eyebrows in a questioning gesture as Jack came in right on cue.

'This one — upstairs front right,' he advised them in what he hoped was a convincing voice of mounting alarm and impending shock, adding, for good measure, 'You took yer bloody time!'

Percy gave the order and four hefty uniformed officers took one webbing handle each as they raced up the front path, pulled their arms back, then rammed the metal bar into the heavy front door, which sagged slightly with a splintering noise, but held.

'Again!' Percy yelled and this time the door floor open, smacking back into the wall of the front hall, narrowly missing the domestic staff member who had been approaching it to investigate the noise. Uniformed constables piled into the hall and Percy ordered them to start at the top of the building and work their way down. An irate figure appeared from a room on the first floor, leaning over the railing in his shirt sleeves, in the process of lifting the braces on his trousers back over his shoulders.

'What the Hell's going on down there? Oh, you,' he added as he spotted Percy in the front hall. 'Didn't we meet in my office?'

'We did indeed, Mr Bradley, and my apologies if there's been some sort of mistake, but we were advised by a gentleman in the street that a lady in here was being strangled to death.'

'Preposterous! What lady, exactly?'

Percy looked up at a uniformed constable who was already on the first landing and yelled up to him. 'Look in the room that this man just came out of!'

The constable disappeared through the door in question and everyone in the house heard the scream and the demand for an explanation. The constable came back out, leaned over the balcony and confirmed Percy's suspicion.

'There's a lady in there right enough, Sergeant. Not a lot of clothes on, but very much alive.'

'I demand an explanation!' Bradley bellowed. 'That lady is my guest and she was taking her afternoon nap. What in God's name is going on?'

'Just doing our duty, Mr Bradley. We had no idea this was your house, of course, but as I said a moment ago, we had a report that a lady was seen through an upstairs window, being strangled by a man. Naturally we had to investigate and so…'

'You've seen the lady in question and she's quite obviously still alive, so take your men and get the Hell out of here, before I contact my very good friend the Police Commissioner.'

'If you're going to do that, sir, then the least I can do is to be able to demonstrate, when questioned, that we made a thorough search of the whole house,' Percy replied.

'This is outrageous!' Bradley bellowed, just as Millicent Mallory appeared at his side, fully clothed, and peered over the balcony at Percy.

'You!' she all but spat, as she turned to speak to Bradley. 'This man came to our house enquiring after that domestic who made off with the twins. A grubby little police person called "Arkwright", or something.'

'Enright,' Percy corrected her. 'This would seem to be an afternoon for coincidences, albeit perhaps unfortunate ones, but clearly you two know each other, since I believe that your husband's in partnership with this gentleman.'

'He most certainly is,' Millicent insisted, 'and I'm here on business.'

'The sort of business that gets discussed in a bedroom?' Percy asked sarcastically.

Millicent bristled. 'How *dare* you, you impudent oaf? What are you inferring?'

'I'm inferring nothing.' Percy grinned up at her, delighted to be able to correct her English. 'I am, however "implying" that the room from which you just emerged is a bedroom and that you and Mr Bradley here were engaging in a "business" as old as Adam and Eve. And to judge by the looks of guilt on both your faces I'm about to "infer" it as well.'

'You disgusting little peasant!' Millicent screamed down at him. 'Just because people behave like that in the pigsty environment in which you were no doubt raised, you have no right to assume it of your betters. You haven't heard the last of this, believe me!'

'I haven't *seen* the last of it, either,' Percy insisted as he walked to the end of the hall and mounted the staircase to where Millicent and Bradley were standing, heading for the open bedroom door. He looked pointedly into it from where the irate couple were blocking his passage and smirked. 'That's the most luxuriously equipped meeting room *I* ever saw and I think I can see the end of a large double bed. May I?'

'No, you may not!' Bradley yelled as he stepped forward and grabbed Percy by his jacket collar. Percy reached up, gripped his hand and twisted, smiling as he heard the bone snap at the same time that he heard Bradley scream in pain.

Percy turned to the uniformed constable still on the landing. 'Book him for obstruction.'

'You bullying bastard!' Millicent screamed as she slapped him hard across the cheek.

'And book her for assaulting a police officer in the course of his duty,' Percy added as he walked into the bedroom, where the pulled back covers and rumpled pillows betrayed what sort of business meeting had been taking place.

He walked back onto the landing and looked down into the hallway, through which Bradley and Millicent were being escorted towards the yawning gap that had once been a front door, in full view of a handful of domestic servants who had gathered in the hallway for the free entertainment.

He walked down the flight of stairs and waited in the hall as one by one the constables came back downstairs to announce that they had found nothing.

'Nothing at all?' he demanded of each of them in turn and as they confirmed that the rooms were empty of people, he began to swear. Then finally, in desperation, he called all the men back down and issued one final instruction. 'Go back up there and search again. Cupboards, wardrobes, under beds, inside desk drawers — anywhere where things might be hidden.'

'What exactly are we looking for, Sergeant?' one of the men asked.

Percy grimaced. 'This may sound ridiculous, but we're looking for two infant boys. Twins, about eighteen months old. You're probably all asking yourselves "How could we possibly have missed them?" but you didn't know then what you were looking for. So, go back and try again.'

As he stood there quietly consoling himself with the fact that he'd at least managed to arrest two very unpleasant people, one of the uniformed maidservants sidled up to him.

'Beggin' yer pardon, officer, but there *was* a couple o' babies 'ere until recently. We never got to see 'em properly, 'cos they was kept upstairs wiv a nursemaid, but they was sent ter the country a few days since an' they 'aven't bin back 'ere.'

'Do you know *where* exactly in the country?' Percy enquired.

'No, sir, but the master 'as this place in Norfolk somewhere.'

'Yes, so I'm advised. Thank you ...?'

'Mary, sir, but don't tell the master that I said owt to yer. Only them's lovely little children an' I'd 'ate ter think o' them separated from their mother.'

Percy called off the ongoing search, then gave instructions for the two prisoners to be driven down to Scotland Yard and placed in separate interrogation rooms. He sent a wire to Norwich police and after thinking deeply while tapping a pencil thoughtfully against his teeth he set off for his first interview.

Victor Bradley was the epitome of outraged dignity as he sat on the other side of the narrow table in the windowless, and almost airless, room, with a uniformed police constable seated next to him.

'I believe that my wrist's broken,' he complained before Percy had even taken a seat, 'and when my solicitor arrives I'll be instructing him to make a formal complaint and file an action for damages. And you can't keep me here forever on a trumped up charge.'

'When — and if — you get to see your solicitor, Mr Bradley, he'll assure you that obstructing a police officer in the course of his duty is an offence that our courts take very seriously. As are corruption in the conduct of a public office and wasting police time. I'm just awaiting confirmation that George and William Mallory have been found safe and well on your Horning estate, then I'll be able to add kidnapping to the list. If they're *not* safe and well, it'll be murder. Twice.'

'Ridiculous!' Bradley asserted. 'Even a bone-headed plod such as you must realise by now that it was never a proper kidnapping. Spencer Mallory planned it, in order to get access to his wife's trust money, which we needed for the development project in Bethnal Green.'

'But from Mr Mallory's perspective, it all went very wrong, didn't it? Why did you not return the children?'

'Have you not even worked that out yet? As you discovered, Millie — Mrs Mallory, that is — and I have been conducting an affair for some years now. She planned on leaving Spencer with those two whining brats that he'd ruined, but she wanted the twins for herself, so we simply slipped that dreadful man Maguire a bit extra to hand the children over to us once he'd gone through the pretence of kidnapping them from that wet girl that the Mallory family employed as their nanny.'

'When did Mrs Mallory learn of the plot to extort the money from her family trust?'

'As soon as I told her what Spencer was planning. We realised that it would be a golden opportunity to get the twins away from Spencer, making it easier when it came to the divorce that she was planning to petition for. So, you see, you can't charge her in connection with the fake kidnapping, because she knew all about it all along and was happy to go along with the pretence that she was desperate to get the twins back.'

'How did you come to engage Mr Maguire's services?'

'He was some lowlife scum that Spencer knew of, who he was already employing to carry out the evictions and rent collections. He was more than happy to earn a little extra for a trip to Hampstead Heath.'

There was a tap on the door and a uniformed sergeant poked his head into the room and gestured with a jerk of his head that he wished to have a word with Percy, who returned to the room two minutes later with a broad smile.

'We've located the twins alive and well, so now it's just the remaining charges.'

'You don't have a hope of making those stick,' Bradley sneered, 'so may I go now?'

'Not just for the moment, Mr Bradley,' Percy smiled back gloatingly. 'We'll just see how well I can make that corruption in public office charge stick when I've taken Mr Mallory the good news regarding the finding of the twins, and the bad news about how they came to be in Norfolk.'

Two rooms down, Millicent Mallory wasn't looking quite so glamorous and the body language between her and the grossly overweight police constable who sat silently next to her was not the most fluent.

'The good news is that we've located your twin sons alive and well, Mrs Mallory,' Percy beamed sarcastically, 'but then you knew all along where they were, didn't you?'

'You can't keep me here like this, in all male company,' Millicent complained. 'It's not seemly and this oaf seems to find my bosom of considerable interest.'

'That's something he has in common with Mr Bradley, of course,' Percy smirked. 'I agree that it would be better if we employed females here in the Met, to act as escorts for female prisoners, but as yet we don't. However, from time to time we find it efficacious to employ females in what you might call "assumed" roles. You've met one of the best already — my nephew's wife, Esther, who's so good with a needle and thread.'

'That's pure dishonesty!' Millicent protested.

Percy nodded. 'Almost as bad as faking the kidnapping of one's own infant children. And before you deny it, Mr Bradley's already obligingly confirmed what I already suspected anyway.'

'It's not an offence to kidnap one's own children, surely?'

'Probably not, but it *is* an offence to defraud the trustees of a family trust, so we've got both you and your husband for that. I gather that Mr Mallory wasn't in on the part of the plan in which you didn't return the children as promised, so we can only charge you and Mr Bradley with that. Assault, false imprisonment or something along those lines.'

'Even your own children?'

'Probably that as well, although that will be a matter for the lawyers. Mr Bradley will be paying a high price for your affections, will he not? Assuming that the divorce goes through — and no-one could deny that your husband would have good grounds after all this — Mr Bradley still seems to have committed himself to bringing up another man's children.'

'They're *his* children, you dolt!' she yelled back at him. 'Had you not worked that out for yourself?'

Percy was taken aback for a moment, but soon regathered his composure.

'No, I must admit that you had me fooled on that particular point of detail. But it just makes the entire bizarre business more credible to a jury. In addition, of course, it will make Mr Mallory all the more determined to have his revenge, when I tell him.'

'You surely don't propose to tell him yourself?' Millicent demanded in an outraged tone.

'Why not?' Percy smiled back as he rose to leave. 'After all, there have to be *some* perks in this job.'

Just over an hour later Percy ignored the protests of the woman behind the front desk as he threw open the door to Mallory's office in The Strand and strode in without an appointment, without an invitation, and without any hesitation. A small middle-aged man with spectacles on the end of his nose looked round in astonishment as Percy jerked his head in an instruction for him to leave.

'What the Hell is the meaning of this?' Mallory demanded. 'This man is my Conveyancing assistant and we're discussing important matters.'

'He may well prove to your replacement as a partner, Mr Mallory,' Percy snarled back. 'Now get him out of here, unless you want what we have to talk about made the subject of office gossip for weeks.'

Mallory nodded for the little man to leave and as he scuttled out Percy took a seat without being invited.

'Despite the preliminary appearances, Mr Mallory, I'm here with some good news. We've found your twin sons and they're unharmed.'

'God be praised!' Mallory said. 'Where were they — in some low den in the East End?'

'No, on an estate in Norfolk. Horning, to be precise. Ring any bells?'

'The only person I know who has land there is my business partner and very good friend Victor Bradley.'

'He's also a very good friend of your wife's, I'm afraid.' Percy couldn't help but smile, as Mallory's face went dark.

'I take it that was some sort of unworthy innuendo? A hint at her marital infidelity with my best friend?'

'A bit of a cliché, isn't it? Which is why I wouldn't have employed it by way of a lie.'

'Where's your proof?'

'I had occasion to visit Mr Bradley's home this afternoon, where your wife was about to take her usual pleasures in lieu of what she told you was her regular appointment at her bridge club. Both he and she were discovered in a state of undress and there was a bedroom on the first floor that appeared to have been recently occupied.'

'That's purely circumstantial.'

'Let's not walk around each other, Mr Mallory. They both confessed to their adultery earlier this afternoon and Mr Bradley was within his rights to have the temporary custody of the twin boys, since they are — according to Mrs Mallory — his.'

Mallory sank back in his chair, his face ashen and his hands trembling. Finally, he found his voice. 'I *had* suspected something for some time, since Millie was — well, she didn't seem to — let's just say that we've had separate bedrooms for some time.'

'Around the time when she conceived the twins?'

'There's no need to rub it in — although that slimy bastard Bradley obviously did. Let me tell you a few things about that double dealing, two-faced hypocritical piece of pond life.'

'I'm all ears.' Percy smiled as he extracted his notebook.

'For a start, the contract in Bethnal Green. We agreed on the formation of the company long before the Council agreed to the Boundary Scheme. It was in fact Bradley who persuaded the Council to go ahead with it, as a trial run for other schemes in the future, except of course that he didn't exactly advise the Council that our company would be making heaps out of it, once we had the existing tenants out. And it was Bradley who produced that disgusting piece of humanity Michael Truegood to play the heavy stuff with those who refused to get out. We obviously, shall we say, "adjusted" the company account to make it look as if Bradley purchased his share in the business at a much later date.'

'I'm not surprised to have the corruption confirmed, but I must admit that I had no idea that Bradley listed Truegood, or rather Maguire, among his friends.'

'He didn't, exactly. Some years ago, when we needed cheap labour for some earthworks out in Essex, where we were building houses, he had this inspiration to contact the local jails in an initiative to recruit prisoners who were about to be released, who were desperate for work. As you know, people are very reluctant to employ those with a prison record and the scheme worked very well, and very economically. During the course of that he got very friendly with a man who went on to be the Deputy Keeper at Newgate.'

'Edmund Tillotson?'

'That's the man. Anyway, when we bought the properties in Bethnal Green and it was obvious that there'd be some resistance to the demolitions, Bradley contacted his old friend, looking for someone who'd be capable of scaring people into moving out. Tillotson came up with Maguire, or "Truegood", as he decided to call himself. He was due to hang anyway and was only too happy to escape the noose with a bit of "inside assistance".'

'So it *was* Tillotson who was behind Maguire's jail break?'

'You'd need to confirm that with Bradley, but that's what he told me. He also said something about Maguire being employed to do away with you when you were getting too close to the truth. Unfortunately, it obviously didn't work.'

'Would you be prepared to testify to all this in court?'

'It depends what it's worth to me.'

Percy thought for a moment and reluctantly came up with a deal.

'If you're prepared to give that evidence, I think I can persuade my superiors that we can restrict the charge against you to one of defrauding your wife's family trust. You probably won't even go to jail, since your lawyer could argue that you'd been punished enough already. I take it that you'll be struck off for defrauding a trust?'

Mallory nodded sadly. 'Indeed, it's difficult to imagine a worse offence by a man in my professional position.'

'I obviously can't promise anything, Mr Mallory, but I'll have a word with the appropriate senior people at the Yard.'

The following morning, after being processed up through the levels, Percy found himself taking tea and biscuits with the Commissioner himself. Alongside him was a Senior Treasury Counsel called Humphreys, who'd been brought in as a consultant on the legal aspects of what Percy was proposing when he indicated in advance that it would be necessary to grant immunities from prosecution to a very prominent man in the legal profession and a former criminal associate of a man who was now dead.

'I hope that what you're about to tell us is as spectacular as you indicated to my aide, Sergeant. I know of your reputation as a hard-hitting and thorough thief-taker, but I'm advised that what you have to disclose is more in the way of a major scandal involving gross corruption in public office. I have a meeting booked with the Home Secretary for three o'clock this afternoon, so I hope that you aren't about to disappoint me.'

'So do I, Commissioner. But it's rather a long and convoluted tale, I'm afraid.'

'You have ten minutes, Sergeant.'

'Very well. It's all centred around what they call the "Boundary Scheme" in Bethnal Green. As you may well be aware, the LCC were under considerable pressure to demolish some of London's worst slums and replace them with decent working-class housing, following that Royal Commission Report.'

'Yes, I think you can assume that I'm familiar with the politics, Sergeant, so just concentrate on the relevant bits.'

'Yes, Commissioner. Well, anyway, Victor Bradley, who's an Assistant at the LCC, with particular responsibility for building and urban planning, had for some years been operating joint venture schemes with a leading West End lawyer called Spencer Mallory — mainly out in Essex, building houses. Then, when various potential locations were identified for these new housing schemes in London itself, the two of them saw Bethnal Green as the most likely and they formed a company to reap the rewards if and when the contract was awarded.'

'Was this company formed before or after the approval of the scheme by the LCC?' Humphreys enquired from over his horn-rimmed spectacles.

'Well before and that's where the corruption begins. Bradley agreed with Mallory that Mallory would float the company and that Bradley would come in as an equal value shareholder, with a buy-in capital of twenty thousand, to match an equal contribution of twenty thousand by Mallory. I haven't yet examined the true company accounts, but Bradley handed me a page from them that tended to suggest that his purchase came long after the award of the contract for the demolition of the existing slums to the company — Gregory Properties, it's called. But Mallory's prepared to testify that the payment from Bradley came much earlier than that, as no doubt the version of accounts held with the bank will confirm. The account sheet that Bradley showed me was just so much window dressing, it would seem.'

'That point will need to be checked,' Humphreys muttered as he made an appropriate note.

'So, if you're correct, Sergeant,' the Commissioner added, 'it would seem that we can prove that Bradley was a shareholder in Gregory Properties long before it received the contract and was therefore well placed to push his own interests when it came to the award of the demolition work. Is that the essence of his corruption?'

'Basically, yes,' Percy confirmed. 'But in terms of criminal activity it gets much worse.'

'Go on,' Humphreys urged him, writing furiously in his notebook.

'Well, as you might well imagine, the residents of the existing slums didn't take too kindly to the suggestion that they might have to move on. Strange as it may seem, those who live in those hovels get very attached to them — literally, if they brush too tightly against the walls — and they began to insist that they were not for moving. By then, Gregory Properties, through Bradley's close friendship with the Deputy Keeper of Newgate, had identified the very man to persuade them to move more urgently once the company had bought a square of hovels right where the Scheme was to be built and installed this man — real name "Maguire", but calling himself "Truegood" — as the rent collector for the time being, until the evictions began.'

'You mentioned to my aide that the corruption extended to Newgate, Sergeant. Are we now getting to that bit?'

'Indeed we are, Commissioner, if you'd just bear with me a while longer. This man Maguire was due to hang for murder some time over a year ago, along with a fellow prisoner called Grieves. But the jail records for that day show only one hanging and thanks to some eagle-eyed detective work by Constable Enright in Records...'

'Your nephew, the one who got the bravery medal recently?'

'The very same, Commissioner. He spotted that the physical description of the man hanged that day fitted Grieves rather than Maguire — they were physically very different — but that according to the jail records, the man who took the drop was Maguire. When I tackled the Deputy Keeper — a man named Tillotson — on that very point, he insisted that the man hanged was Maguire and that Grieves had suicided at roughly the same time. All those who die in Newgate are buried with a heavy dose of quicklime to hasten the decomposition, of course, so it was no use by then ordering the disinterment of Grieves.'

'You're suggesting that this man Tillotson faked the jail records and then allowed Maguire to slip away unnoticed?' Humphreys interposed.

Percy nodded, while the Commissioner allowed himself a low whistle.

'You weren't exaggerating were you, Sergeant?'

'Indeed not, but there's more.'

'We already have enough to prosecute both Tillotson and Bradley,' Humphreys confirmed.

Percy shrugged his shoulders in a 'maybe' gesture. 'That's where I need the immunities, Mr Humphries. We only have Mallory's evidence to prove that the buy-in by Bradley came *before* the contract was awarded to Gregory Properties. We can't prosecute Mallory *and* rely on his evidence against Bradley at one and the same time.'

'He wouldn't be the first to employ a "cut-throat" defence against a fellow accused, but I get your point,' Humphreys replied with a knitted brow. 'Leave that point with me. But where's our evidence against Tillotson? Was that his name, the jail person?'

'That's him — Deputy Keeper at Newgate. However, I took the precaution of arranging another jail break, this time netting Maguire himself as the man behind it. Along with Maguire we nabbed a man called Venables who was in on the entire thing and can point the finger at Tillotson when he goes to trial for his part in the break-out of a woman called Martha Crabbe, who unfortunately got away in all the confusion at the main gate of Newgate.'

'Why can't we use this man Maguire for the same purpose?' Humphreys enquired.

Percy faked a grimace. 'Unfortunately, he's dead — done to death by a street mob in a most embarrassing incident outside Bethnal Green Police Station while he was being transferred to a paddy wagon to take him back to Newgate.'

'According to the Inspector down there, you deliberately arranged for that to happen, Sergeant,' the Commissioner interrupted him. 'I have a very adverse report against you here on my desk and if you hadn't coincidentally asked to see me today, I'd have been taking that point up with you. Whatever the truth of the matter, we no longer have Maguire, is that what you're telling us?'

'Correct, Commissioner.'

'And you want an immunity for this Venables chappie?' Humphreys added. 'That shouldn't be too difficult, if the current charge is a simple one of facilitating a prison escape and the prize is the prosecution of its Deputy Keeper.'

'With respect, Mr Humphreys, we need more than that and in a sense *less* than that.'

'Don't talk in riddles, man!' the Commissioner demanded. 'You've already exceeded your ten minutes, by the way, but this is so fascinating that I'm prepared to run late for my next appointment. Carry on, but be brief.'

'Well, to keep it brief,' Percy continued, 'Venables wasn't just in on the jail break. He was present during a series of five murders in Bethnal Green when Maguire decided to demonstrate to those who were wavering about moving on that their immediate health might depend upon it.'

'He murdered five people in order to put the frighteners on the waverers, you mean?' Humphreys asked.

Percy nodded again. 'Exactly. Venables assures me that he was simply there to make up the numbers and that Maguire did the actual murders and I have no reason to doubt him. But we can hardly expect Mr Venables to confess to five capital crimes and we need Venables's statement — which I've already secured — in order to close the book on five murders and assure the good people of Bethnal Green that the reign of terror is over. That, plus the very public spectacle of Mr Maguire going to his maker under a pile of rocks hurled by the mob.'

'So, you want to prosecute Venables just for his part in the jail break?' Humphries asked.

Again, Percy nodded. 'Yes, and he's happy to plead guilty to that if we drop the rest. Plus, of course, he can testify against Tillotson, along with a very frightened turnkey who got his orders direct from Tillotson and would sell his own grandmother rather than become a prisoner in his former place of employment. He knows what the conditions are like in there, of course, and he's terrified of being locked into one of those communal cells with people he's brutalised in the past from behind the safety of a set of bars.'

Humphries looked sideways at the Commissioner and nodded. 'I'm sure I'll be able to persuade the Attorney-General to go along with what the Sergeant here's requesting. Congratulations, Sergeant, you've served the people of London most royally. Now if you'll excuse me, Commissioner, I have to be at the Old Bailey by lunchtime.'

The Commissioner signalled for Percy to remain where he was while he escorted Humphries to the door, then came back and sat staring at Percy for a long silent moment.

'You don't entirely fool me, Sergeant, and there are times when your devious way of going about things scares the Hell out of senior officers here at the Yard. But you get results and it may be that we can use your talents for underhand manoeuvres and total disregard for regulations and protocol. I take it that you've completed your work down in Bethnal Green?'

'More or less, Commissioner.'

'Well get yourself back here, take a couple of days off and await further developments. And tell that nephew of yours that he'll soon be back on two legs.'

Chapter Eighteen

'Oi, you!' Sergeant Ballantyne yelled as Jack did his best to slip a pile of completed Crime Summaries onto the sweetie counter without being spotted. 'Where was yer yesterday afternoon?'

'Out,' Jack replied evasively while cursing himself for not having a story ready to explain his collaboration with Uncle Percy in the well lined streets of Kentish Town.

'Obviously "out", yer dodgy skilamalink. Out where, exactly?'

'Kentish Town, Sergeant.'

'Takin' afternoon tea wi' the minor nobility, was yer?'

'No, Sergeant — assisting in an enquiry.'

'What, an enquiry as ter 'ow many beers yer could sink?'

'No, a proper police enquiry. You'll no doubt be hearing about it soon.'

'An' *you'll* no doubt be 'earin' pretty soon that yer out've 'ere on yer arse. I've given yer the benefit o' too many doubts already an' now yer in trouble. My report goes in this mornin' an' then yer can expect ter be makin' a trip down ter the casual labour queue in the docks. Don't fancy yer chances, though, wi' only one leg. But yer finished in 'ere, so don't bother takin' up a valuable space down the corridor there. Just bugger off 'ome an' tell yer wife that she'll be takin' in washin' ter keep yer both fed.'

Jack wandered disconsolately back down the hallway to say goodbye to his colleagues. The one bright light on his horizon was the fact that Tim Kilmore appeared to be no longer preparing to grow tomatoes round his head and Jack smiled encouragingly as he opted to steal a couple of pencils from the supply on his former desk.

'Morning, Tim,' he said. 'They cut your picture frame off, I see.'

Tim smiled back happily. 'At least my young lady can kiss me again and the other good news is that I've been sent back to general duties with effect from the first Monday of next month. Sergeant Ballantyne's looking for you, by the way.'

'He found me, unfortunately,' Jack grimaced, 'and I got my marching orders.'

'Tough luck,' Tim commiserated, 'but you *have* been taking rather a lot of time off lately. Will you be paid till the end of the week?'

'No idea. I was just told to go home and await official notification that I'm no longer employed in the Met.'

'Have you got any other plans?'

'Apart from slashing my wrists, no. I'm just dreading telling my wife.'

'Good luck anyway,' Tim replied. 'I'm going to miss you — and *this* place, funnily enough. Now it's back to being sworn and spat at and mixing it with all the riff-raff that we have to arrest.'

'Half your luck,' Jack muttered as he turned to go. 'For once, having a sergeant for an uncle didn't save me.'

Back at home he announced the gloomy tidings to Esther as they sat at the tea table.

Esther put her arm over his shoulder and kissed him.

'At least I'll have you home more often. But as soon as Uncle Percy gets here I'll have to leave you with Alice, when she comes down. I wasn't expecting you home, obviously, so I asked Alice to mind the children while I go off on this babysitting expedition of my own that Uncle Percy seems to have all planned for me. Bethnal Green this time — I hope it's a bit better than its reputation.'

'Will you have time for dinner before you go?' Jack said solicitously and Esther smirked back at him.

'Have you learned to cook?'

'I was thinking of sandwiches. I could make some for Alice too. Are there any biscuits in the tin?'

'Yes, and I've counted them. Alice normally takes only one with her tea and you're allowed two. There had better be seven left when I get back.'

'And when will that be?'

'No idea, but leave Alice to bathe the children and put them to bed. We don't want to be accused of child neglect.'

'That's someone at the door.'

'I know — I haven't gone deaf. Let's have a guessing competition.'

'An extra biscuit says it's Uncle Percy.'

'One less biscuit says that it's Alice.'

'You just did me out of a biscuit,' Jack complained gloomily as he opened the door to a surprised looking Alice.

'I wasn't expecting you to be home,' she said. 'Only Esther said she had to go out on some business with your uncle and she wanted me to look after the children. But if you're going to be home anyway…'

'Even if Jack *is* home,' Esther advised her with a grin as she walked down the hallway, 'the children still need to be left in the care of a responsible adult. He's only allowed one biscuit, by the way — oh, here comes the man who's going to take me for a lightening spin around the East End.'

'Thoughtful of you to hire a cab,' Esther commented as she and Percy headed south down Aldersgate Street. 'This must be quite important; either that, or you're trying to butter me up for an unpleasant encounter.'

'It *is* very important, in a way. We're on our way to Bethnal Green Police Station, where you'll be meeting a girl calling herself "Clara". She'll be very dirty and malodorous when they bring her up from the cells, but she's committed no crime you need worry about and I want you to spend that money I gave you on getting her cleaned up and respectable looking. Then I want you to take her home with you — I'll be waiting there to explain everything.'

'I think you should know that Jack was fired today,' Esther advised him gloomily, 'so if you're thinking that we can employ this girl in some sort of domestic role, then forget it, quite apart from the fact that we don't have a spare room for a servant.'

'Jack was only fired from Records,' Percy assured her with a smile, 'and unless Uncle Percy has lost his influence where it matters in the Yard, that was the best career move he ever made. As for the accommodation, I think you'll find that will be taken care of as well.'

'You love weaving your little mysteries, don't you?' Esther smiled despite herself. 'Are you going to tell me anything more about this Clara girl?'

'See what you can find out for yourself,' Percy replied mysteriously. 'I've said it before and I'll keep repeating it until someone listens and acts upon it — you're a natural detective and as soon as the Yard starts recruiting females, I'm putting your name forward.'

'You're the world's greatest flatterer too, when it suits your purpose,' Esther grinned, 'but I want it understood that I'm only doing this to help a poor East End girl just like I used to be. I consider myself so lucky to have met Jack and been afforded a decent life outside Spitalfields and if I can help to give the same change of fortune to another girl about the age I was then, I'll simply be repaying my debt to God. Is that a tear in your eye, Uncle Percy?'

'Nonsense, just some grit. We're almost there, so take a deep breath.'

Thirty minutes later Esther had been introduced to Clara, who took one look at Esther's immaculate make-up and neatly coiled back hair and apologised for the state she was in.

'I don't always smell this disgustin',' she assured Esther, 'an' I bin livin' in these clothes fer two weeks, I'm sorry.'

'Nothing to apologise for,' Esther assured her, 'and by supper time you won't recognise yourself. First of all, we're off to Poplar — ever been there?'

'A couple o' times, but why today?'

'Well, don't get all embarrassed, but there's a public bathhouse there and once you're all clean again we can see about your hair. Do you have a home to go back to briefly and any clothes in storage somewhere?'

'My old boyfriend's mother still 'as some o' me clothes, but she's in Shoreditch,' Clara replied.

'Well, we *are* going to be busy then, aren't we?' Esther replied breezily. 'Let's step outside and find a coach.'

Two hours later, there was no recognising Clara as she smiled happily from under her newly sculpted hairdo, smelling faintly of the bath oil that she'd been handed by Esther on her way into the public bathhouse and wearing her favourite blue dress and black lace-up boots over a brand new set of undergarments that Esther had helped her to select in a local ladies' outfitters shop in Shoreditch. Now they were heading

154

back north towards Clerkenwell and Esther was hoping that Jack hadn't got too much under Alice's feet and that the children had not made him any gloomier with their behaviour.

'That house in Shoreditch where you'd stored your clothes,' Esther prompted her, 'did you say it belonged to your former boyfriend's mother?'

'Yes, that's right,' Clara confirmed.

'Was your former boyfriend there when you went inside?' Esther probed further, having remained inside the hired coach while Clara had gone in.

'No — 'e were murdered a few weeks since,' Clara replied gloomily.

Esther searched inside her handbag for the pencil and paper that she always kept there, wrote something down and slipped the note into her jacket pocket.

'What yer writin' down?' Clara asked.

Esther smiled reassuringly. 'Nothing for you to worry about; just something to prove to that lovely Sergeant Enright that he was correct in his assessment of me.'

'Where we 'eadin'?'

'Clerkenwell — you're coming home with me, to meet my lovely husband and children.'

'I know *two* people in Clerkenwell now.' Clara smiled and Esther was more confident about what she had written on the note.

Back home, Jack had been reminded that playing with his son and daughter was a pleasant way of whiling away an afternoon and had seen first-hand why Esther preferred Alice as her babysitter. Percy had been back for several hours and had assured Jack that he would make a full confession to Esther regarding the number of biscuits he'd consumed.

The children had already been washed and put to bed in their nightclothes when they all heard the sound of the key in the front door and Percy leapt to his feet and scuttled into the hallway, closing the kitchen door on his way out, leaving Jack and Alice still inside it with puzzled expressions. He advanced down the hall to where Esther was almost dragging a nervous looking Clara inside.

'When she saw the house number on the wall, she didn't want to come in,' Esther grinned, 'and I think I know why.' She extracted the note from her jacket and handed it to Percy. 'I'm right, aren't I?' she gloated.

Percy raised his eyes in surprise and hugged her around the shoulder.

'You'll *definitely* be my first recruit,' he advised her warmly. 'So intelligent *and* so beautiful. I just hope that Jack realises how lucky he is.'

'You might want to remind him occasionally,' Esther chuckled, then nodded towards the kitchen door. 'Have you imprisoned them *both* in there?'

Percy nodded and turned to speak to Clara. 'Clara, my dear, in a few seconds you can revert to your real name, but both you and someone else are in for a big surprise. Just take my hand and come with me.'

He led the reluctant girl down the hall and opened the kitchen door. Then with a big self-satisfied smirk he stood to one side and announced, 'It's a few months short of Christmas, but here's an early present for Alice.'

Alice stood up in shocked silence. Her jaw dropped and she burst into howls of tears as she raced forward and hugged their visitor. Barely coherent, the words came tumbling out in chokes and gasps.

'Emily! Beautiful! God. Prayers. Emily! Love you! Going to pass out, I think.'

Jack grabbed Alice's arm and lowered her into a chair.

'Is there one fer me?' Emily gurgled as the tears ran down her face and Alice grabbed her arm and pulled her down on her knee as they both bawled like babies, their arms wrapped around each other.

Esther smirked as she looked sideways at Percy. 'There's no grit in my kitchen, so think of some other excuse this time.'

Once Alice and Emily had calmed down and were sat side by side holding hands, Emily looked up at Percy.

''Ow did yer know?'

'Well, I knew that you weren't Clara Manders, because she was killed by Maguire and his thugs. I didn't know that until after I'd had you locked away for your own safety and then I began to ask myself who you *really* were. You seemed to know all about the kidnapping of the children and the body left in the rubble who everyone supposed had been you. But then I remembered that when you'd been brought up to see me in my office, you were walking with a limp.'

'I told the Sergeant here that you walked with a limp and that's how the body came to be formally identified as you,' Alice explained.

'That's where I was guilty of carelessness,' Percy admitted. 'I was so anxious to prevent Alice having to identify a very unpleasant corpse that I settled for a second-hand identification and I relied on the fact that the girl whose body was found in the rubble in Short Street had probably walked with a limp because she'd suffered a broken ankle in the past.'

'That were Clara Manders, o' course,' Emily explained. 'The poor thing tried to climb onto the top of the church roof when she was nine, in order ter be closer ter God, an' she slipped ter the ground.'

'And I added to the confusion by only asking Alice if Emily had walked with a limp,' Jack admitted, 'without asking her to describe the limp more fully.'

'I were born wi' a slightly displaced 'ip.' Emily smiled. 'It's troubled me all me life, but I never thought it'd lead to me bein' taken fer a dead body.'

'Anyway, it's all sorted now,' Alice beamed, 'and you can come and live with me.'

Emily's face fell. 'There's summat else yer should know about me,' she said in a small voice. 'I think I may be pregnant.'

Contrary to Emily's expectations, Alice clapped her hands with joy. 'Perfect! I didn't think that God could bring me any more joy in one day, but to have a little one to look after all these years would be a gift from the heavens! *Do* please say you'll come and live with me and have the baby under my roof!'

More tears rolled down Emily's face as she reached out and hugged Alice to her. 'Dear Aunty Alice — yer such a wonderful person!'

'Nonsense, girl,' Alice replied, 'it's just that I need someone to look after. From being a lonely old widow living alone, I've suddenly got a niece and a baby that need me. You've no idea how much that means until you've experienced loneliness.'

'Before any of this can happen,' Percy reminded them, 'I need to be satisfied that Emily's committed no crimes that I'm obliged to report. I'm almost certain that she hasn't, but let's start with the kidnapping of the children. I take it you weren't involved in the planning of that?'

'Course not,' Emily replied indignantly. 'I were walkin' them in the Park that day an' a couple o' blokes come from be'ind some bushes an' said that they was takin' the children an' that I was ter come wiv 'em. I were terrified, 'specially when they took us all in this wagon ter this big 'ouse somewhere in this posh neighbour'ood an' that 'orrible Mangler appeared outa nowhere an' told me ter get lost. That's when I ran back ter Tommy.'

'But you didn't report what had happened?' Percy asked.

Emily shook her head. 'I were too frightened, 'specially when Tommy told me that Mangler were the one who'd killed me Dad the previous year. 'E told me that 'e'd told the coppers about that an' that Mangler were gonna be arrested an' that then it'd be safe ter tell 'em where the children was bein' kept. Then Tommy got murdered an' Mangler showed up an' told me that I'd be next, unless I give 'im me 'andbag an' sent a message fer you ter meet me at that 'ouse where Mangler tried ter kill yer an' I got arrested meself. I'm right sorry about that, by the way.'

'No need to apologise,' Percy assured her, 'since you warned me with your eyes. Was that deliberate?'

'I can't remember, ter be honest wi' yer, but I'm right glad yer 'ad that gun 'andy.'

'I'd be dead now, if I hadn't,' Percy smiled reminiscently, 'but that explains how your handbag came to be near Clara Manders's body.'

'Mangler did fer 'er the night before,' Emily advised him. 'I knew she were dead an' that folks would think it were me, so when I got arrested I just pretended I was 'er.'

'The baby you're expecting is Tommy's?' Esther asked.

Emily nodded tearfully. 'Yeah, but 'e never knew, 'cos I weren't sure then. But if it's a boy I'll call 'im Tommy.'

It fell silent, then Jack enquired, 'Is anybody else feeling hungry?'

'Don't tell me that it's my turn for the surprise of the decade and Jack's about to offer to cook?' Esther grinned. 'Mind you, after all the biscuits he seems to have consumed, I'm surprised he's got any room left for supper.'

'It's time for my confession,' Percy volunteered, as Jack stared hard at him. 'I ate four while you were in Bethnal Green, so Jack's off the hook. As for supper, who fancies fish and chips?'

'You were told to take two days off, then come back here and await further instructions,' the Commissioner complained as Percy took a seat. 'We sent men to your home, by the way, and your wife probably thinks that you're with your fancy woman somewhere.'

Percy grinned. 'I'll be fifty-four next year, so I think my wife knows better than to suspect me of sexual excitement. I was down at Newgate, arresting its Deputy Keeper.'

'Well, now you're here, I want to discuss something with you that's directly related to that and concerns your immediate future.'

'I don't see myself having a career in the Prison Service,' Percy smiled, 'so how can I be of further assistance at the Yard?'

'Well, it's like this. Your uncovering of the corruption in the LCC and Newgate has given the Home Secretary food for thought. As you'll know, if you read the newspapers, there's a lot of political unrest in the nation at present and London's the obvious focal point for it, given that we have Parliament House here. There's that idiot woman Fawcett insisting that women should have a greater say in how the nation's run and the Irish are constantly muttering about forming their own country, free of English rule. Then there are all those scandals that the Prince of Wales keeps getting himself into with that Marlborough House set and — well, you get my drift.'

'Indeed, Commissioner, but until they commit criminal offences...'

'That's just the point, Sergeant — *until* they commit criminal offences. When they do the nation's in uproar and we need some way of stepping in before it reaches that stage.'

'Isn't that what "spies" are for?'

'If it involves a foreign power, certainly. But who do we have available if it's *only* a domestic matter?'

'I think I begin to understand what the Home Secretary has in mind.' Percy smiled. 'A branch of the Met with its own domestic spies.'

'They wouldn't be called that, obviously,' the Commissioner corrected him. 'It would be simply a special department within the Yard, named the "Political Branch", or something similar and you seem to have demonstrated a talent for worming your way inside criminal activities that smack of corruption in public office.'

'You want me to join this new branch?' Percy enquired.

'No, I want you to *head* it, with the rank of Inspector at this early stage. I can let you have a staff of three or four and within reason you can pick your own team. They have to be prepared to come off the street and sit at desks for longer than most of them are accustomed to and they have to have a nose for ferreting out potential scandals before they happen, by reading between the lines of routine reports.'

'You're placing a lot of trust in me,' Percy pointed out, 'and there are some in the Met who regard my methods as a bit — shall we say "unusual"?'

'Why do you think you came immediately to mind when Asquith came up with the idea? You know how to break rules, you have a talent for getting up official noses, and you don't stand for any nonsense, even from me. So, what do you say?'

Percy thought for a moment, then his face broke into another smile. 'Beatrice *will* be pleased. She's been going on at me for us to move out into Essex somewhere. And I can pick my own team?'

'Within limits, as I said.'

'Only it just so happens that I know someone with recent Records experience who won't be best placed to go racing up and down streets for the immediate future.'

'You have to let him get it occasionally, or else he'll grow tired of the game,' Alice explained to Jack and Lily as they sat playing 'throw the ball over Bertie's head' in the children's room.

'Maybe you should take over,' Jack suggested as he got up from his knees and sat on the chair beside Lily's bed. Alice willingly replaced him and gave Lily a subtle nod every time that Bertie was allowed to catch the ball with an excited chortle.

'How's Emily settling in?' he asked.

Alice smiled. 'Very well. We're going shopping this afternoon and I'm going to spoil her rotten with new clothes for her wardrobe. Her late mother was my younger sister and there are times I swear it's like being with her all over again. I can't thank you enough for what you did.'

'Thank Percy and Esther, not me,' Jack replied modestly.

'Have you any idea what you're going to do for a living, now that you're no longer a policeman?' Alice asked tactfully.

Jack sighed. 'Absolutely no idea, I'm afraid. Policing's all I ever wanted to do and I never bothered much with schooling beyond the basics. I never learned a trade either and all the job openings in London these days seem to involve building.'

'I'm sure something will come up, you'll see,' Alice reassured him. 'God has a way of repaying one kindness with another and if it were in my power to reward you with a new career, I'd be only too happy to oblige.'

'There's tea and uncle in the kitchen,' Esther chirped as she poked her head round the door. 'Best grab a biscuit before Percy scoffs the lot.'

'I didn't hear you come in,' Jack commented as he walked into the kitchen and nodded in Percy's direction.

'Many a burglar's discovered to his cost that I could be stealthier than him,' Percy grinned. Esther shot him a warning look and shook her head, but Percy was not in the mood for either subtlety or sympathy. 'Your beautiful lady wife is trying to warn me not to mention police work, because of what is no doubt your ongoing belief that you and the Yard have parted company. I take it that your discharge letter hasn't come through yet?'

'No,' Jack said, 'but I'm expecting it by every post.'

'I have a letter here for you,' Percy announced solemnly. 'It's from the Met and since I was planning on coming to see you anyway, they asked me to deliver it.'

'Thanks,' Jack muttered as he took it from Percy's outstretched hand and threw it on the table.

'You've learned nothing from me, have you?' Percy grinned.

'Meaning?'

'Meaning that time when you took the trouble to look more carefully at that company account page that Victor Bradley handed me. The one I'd not read properly and that turned out to contain the key to the kidnapping when examined more carefully.'

'So?'

'Open that envelope and read its contents before you make any assumptions.'

'If he won't, I will,' Esther announced as she grabbed the envelope and tore it open. Her eyes ran down the page, before her lips opened in a wide grin and she walked across to where Jack was sitting.

'My second new hat in the same year!' she laughed as she kissed Jack fully on the lips and forced the letter into his hand.

Jack read the letter and his mouth opened wide in delight.

'I've finally been promoted to Sergeant!' he yelled.

'I think the two of us already knew that,' Percy reminded him with a broad grin. 'But there's a catch.'

Jack re-read the letter. 'What's this "Political Branch"? Is it new?'

'So new that it hasn't formally been announced yet. But rumour around the Yard is that it's headed by an Inspector who's a total bastard — pardon me, my dear — who drives his men mercilessly, involves their families in police matters, breaks every rule in the book and regards authority as a personal challenge.'

'Sounds like you.' Jack smiled. Then the smile froze when he saw Percy's idiotic grin. 'Oh my God — it *is* you, isn't it?'

'Indeed it is, so show some respect and pass me the biscuit tin.'

Esther giggled in sheer delight and began kissing Jack with a passion that caused Percy to look away in embarrassment. 'A new hat to go with some more maternity gowns!'

'I'd no idea you'd fallen pregnant again,' Jack responded breathlessly between kisses.

'You should have done,' she grinned back at him. 'You were there at the time.'

A NOTE TO THE READER

I hope that you enjoyed the fourth novel in the Esther and Jack series!

As usual, this novel has real-life events as its background. The 'Old Nichol' ghetto in what is modern Bethnal Green really did exist, and really was demolished in the final years of Victoria's reign, to make way for the very first experiment in public housing anywhere in the world. It was called 'The Boundary Estate', and in due course it become a slum of its own, although it was 'home' to highly successful Londoners such as brothers Lew Grade and Bernard Delfont. You may still connect with the original slums in a very physical way, by standing on the bandstand in the centre of Arnold Circus, a raised mound originally constructed from the 'infill' rubble of the Old Nichol.

London has always possessed slums, even in Roman times. But as life moved on, the slums acquired a different look, and it was a constant battle to provide new and 'better' housing for its rapidly growing population, whose teeming hordes threatened to explode into the streets, where many of them were forced to live anyway. By the 1890s the newly formed London County Council had inherited the responsibilities of the former Metropolitan Board of Works, and the populace were being eagerly advised by the politicians that the scandals that had become synonymous with urban redevelopment were at an end.

But every well-meaning and slightly condescending scheme 'for the betterment of the poor' has its opportunities for corruption, and the demolition of the infamous rookery of verminous dwellings known as 'The Old Nichol' to make way for the much needed, and long-awaited, 'Boundary Estate' proved to be no exception.

This novel, with Jack hobbling around on crutches, also reminds us of the physical risks still faced in their working lives by modern police officers, and the anxiety of the wives who wait at home while their husbands provide for them in a world full of bad people. These days, of course, the 'thin blue line' contains female officers, and there is no need for emancipated women such as Esther to work without formal recognition, although those of them with children have even more cause to be apprehensive of what may be awaiting them around the next corner.

As ever, I'd be delighted to receive your feedback, in addition to your requests regarding what the Enrights should tackle next. In the next novel they will be back in London, but always happy to pack their bags and move on somewhere else. I would be delighted if you could post a review up on **Amazon** or **Goodreads**. Or, of course, you can try the more personal approach on my website, and my Facebook page: **DavidFieldAuthor**.

Happy reading!

David

davidfieldauthor.com

Sapere Books is an exciting new publisher of brilliant fiction and popular history.

To find out more about our latest releases and our monthly bargain books visit our website:
saperebooks.com

Printed in Great Britain
by Amazon